Marrying Harriet

Also by Marion Chesney

ANIMATING MARIA
FINESSING CLARISSA
ENLIGHTENING DELILAH
PERFECTING FIONA
REFINING FELICITY
RAINBIRD'S REVENGE
THE ADVENTURESS
RAKE'S PROGRESS
THE WICKED GODMOTHER
PLAIN JANE
THE MISER OF MAYFAIR
FREDERICA IN FASHION
DIANA THE HUNTRESS
DAPHNE
DEIRDRE AND DESIRE
THE TAMING OF ANNABELLE
MINERVA
REGENCY GOLD
DAISY
ANNABELLE
THE CONSTANT COMPANION
MY DEAR DUCHESS
HENRIETTA
THE MARQUIS TAKES A BRIDE
LADY MARGERY'S INTRIGUES

Marrying Harriet

Marion Chesney

St. Martin's Press
New York

WITHDRAWN

Jefferson-Madison
Regional Library
Charlottesville, Virginia

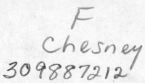

MARRYING HARRIET. Copyright © 1990 by Marion Chesney.
All rights reserved. Printed in the United States of America.
No part of this book may be used or reproduced in any manner
whatsoever without written permission except in the case of
brief quotations embodied in critical articles or reviews. For
information, address St. Martin's Press, 175 Fifth Avenue,
New York, N.Y. 10010.

Library of Congress Cataloging-in-Publication Data

Chesney, Marion.
    Marrying Harriet / Marion Chesney.
      p. cm.
    ISBN 0-312-04276-0
    I. Title.
    PR6053.H4535M35 1990
    823'.914—dc20   89-70339
                                CIP

First Edition
10 9 8 7 6 5 4 3 2 1

Jefferson-Madison
Regional Library
Charlottesville, Virginia

Marrying Harriet

Chapter 1

You will and you won't—You'll be damned if
you do—And you'll be damned if you don't.

—*Lorenzo Dow*

*M*ISS HARRIET BROWN SAT at her desk and pulled a blank sheet of paper towards her. When she was troubled, she wrote down her thoughts, putting the benefits on one side of the page and the problems on the other.

The situation she found herself in was this. Her mother had died giving birth to her. Her father, a Methodist minister, had recently died. Her aunt, Lady Owen, a Scarborough *grande dame* who had cut off her sister, Lydia, when she had stooped low enough to marry plain Mr. Brown, had decided to take care of Harriet—or rather to arrange care for her. To that end, Harriet was being sent to London to live with two professional chaperones, the

Tribble sisters. These sisters were to school her in the ways of society and find her a husband.

On the plus side were the following facts: She, Harriet, had practically no money. The very house she was sitting in belonged to the church and would fall into the hands of the new minister, due to arrive the following week. Marriage was the only future open to her. Although highly educated, she had not the necessary accomplishments expected in a governess—that is, knowledge of Italian, of water-colour painting, dancing, and pianoforte playing. Therefore she should be grateful to her aunt for giving her this opportunity and supplying her with a modest dowry. In London—*even* in London—there might be some worthy, decent man to marry.

On the problem side lay the Tribble sisters. Harriet read the London newspapers in the circulating library and had heard of the Tribbles. They were remarkably successful in finding husbands for "problem" girls. Harriet had been designated a problem by her aunt because she lacked refinement and at twenty-five had considerable experience of good works and none of the ballroom or saloon. Amy and Effy Tribble seemed a shocking pair, however successful they might be. They had punched each other openly at a ball, a murder had been committed in their house, and there was a malicious tale in one of the columns of gossip hinting that Amy Tribble had dressed up as a man and challenged the Duke of Berham to a duel. The fact that this duke had eloped with the Tribbles' latest charge, a Miss Maria Kendall, did not reassure Harriet. It looked as if both Miss Kendall and the duke had been fleeing the Tribble sisters.

Harriet returned to the plus column. Her father, with her help, had managed to save many brands from the burning. If the Tribble sisters needed saving, then it was Harriet's duty to do so.

She was to travel alone on the mail coach from York, Lady Owen's carriage taking her only as far as there. Nor had Lady Owen found it necessary to supply Harriet with a maid or any female companion for the journey. That was definitely a plus, thought Harriet. She could pass the time reading, something she had had little chance to do in recent years with all the work of the parish.

Telling herself she felt much better, Harriet firmly read over what she had written, tore up the paper and dropped it in the waste-paper bucket at her feet. All she lacked was courage and that would come from God.

But as she climbed into Lady Owen's carriage the next day, she felt a lump rising in her throat. Not one of her father's old parishioners had come to see her off. Harriet did not know that the father whose memory she loved and respected had been a highly unpopular man whose harsh, autocratic brand of charity had been accepted out of sheer necessity. She felt very lonely and lost, as if she had no roots anywhere. Behind her stood the grim, cold, uncomfortable house in which she had spent her life to date, closed and shuttered as if it, too, was glad to see the back of her. Ahead of her lay unknown London.

The carriage made its way first to Lady Owen's. Lady Owen came down the steps of her mansion as Harriet stepped down from the coach to say her goodbyes. Lady Owen was a sour, petulant woman with great bushy eyebrows under the eaves of which a pair of pale, cold eyes looked with disdain on the world in general and Harriet Brown in particular.

"Good heavens, child!" exclaimed Lady Owen. "Is that all you have to wear?"

Harriet flushed. She was wearing mourning: black wool gown, large black bonnet, and thick-soled boots.

"These are my mourning clothes," she said quietly.

"Never mind," sighed Lady Owen. "Those Tribbles

have been instructed to furnish you with a new wardrobe." She gave a sour laugh. "At least you will not be troubled by any warm attentions from the gentlemen on your road south."

"My father always said, 'Handsome is as handsome does,' " said Harriet.

"Well, he would, wouldn't he?" sniffed Lady Owen. "And more fool he."

For one moment, Harriet's eyes sparkled and then she quickly reminded herself of her situation. Besides, her father always used to say, 'Sticks and stones may break my bones, but names can never hurt me,' although, thought Harriet with a first flash of disloyalty, there were some remarks that left you feeling physically abused.

"Now restore the name of Owen by marrying well," admonished Lady Owen.

"My name is Brown," pointed out Harriet.

"The name of Brown was but a hiccup in the famous line of Owen," said Lady Owen severely. "On your road, and write to me every week. The Tribbles will frank your letters, for I am paying them enough as it is. You may kiss me."

Harriet screwed up her eyes and pecked Lady Owen on the cheek, recoiling slightly as one of those horrendous eyebrows brushed her face. "If I ever have eyebrows like that, I shall *shave* them," thought Harriet Brown, unaware that that was one of the first worldly thoughts that had entered her head. She was usually firmly of the belief that to embellish one's appearance was flying in the face of God.

She climbed into the coach, but by the time it moved off, Lady Owen had turned and walked back indoors.

The weather was chilly and she was glad, on reaching the coaching inn at York, to find that Lady Owen had

4

booked an inside seat for her. Harriet had heard stories of wild young men who rode the mail coaches, often bribing the coachman to take the ribbons and terrorizing the passengers. But the other passengers looked very sedate. There was an elderly doctor, his wife, a vicar, and a young, fashionably dressed matron and a wide-eyed little boy. Harriet smiled on the little boy, who stuck out his tongue at her when no one else was looking. Harriet glared at him awfully and turned her attention to the bustle in the inn-yard.

The minster clock boomed out six o'clock and the coach moved off. Harriet had never travelled at such speed before. She found it exhilarating. She felt like dancing and singing and wondered what had come over her. After some time, when darkness fell, she became used to the speed and fell asleep. She slept in fits and starts through the night and came fully awake as a red dawn broke on the horizon and they slowed their headlong pace to stop at an inn where they were to have breakfast.

As was the custom, the insiders were fed first and then the outsiders, that is, the people travelling on the roof of the coach.

Harriet was just finishing her breakfast when the child, Jeremy, who was travelling in the coach and whom Harriet had damned as rude and spoilt, burst into the coffee room of the inn, tears running down his face.

"Cat uppa tree," he gasped. "Got to save kitty."

"Now, now, Jeremy," said his mother. "Cats can get down from trees all by themselves."

The passengers, who were all heartily sick of Jeremy, averted their gaze.

"It'll die," screamed Jeremy, punching his mother with his small fists.

His mother, a Mrs. Oakes, looked plaintively round at

the other passengers. "Perhaps some gentleman . . . ?" she said weakly.

But the gentlemen continued eating and ignored her. Jeremy's screams were ear-splitting.

Harriet threw down her napkin and got to her feet. "Stop that noise," she said firmly to Jeremy. "It will do nothing to help the cat. Take me out and show me where it is."

Jeremy stopped screaming and seized her hand and all but dragged her from the inn.

At the bottom of the inn garden was a tall pine tree, a very tall pine tree. And right at the top was the figure of a cat. It mewed dismally.

Harriet looked up at the tree. It was tall and straight, with no lower branches to hold on to. "There is no one among the passengers agile enough to get up there," she said. "Come back to the inn with me, Jeremy, and I shall try to see if one of the servants will go for us."

But the servants refused to budge and the landlord said crossly he was too busy to allow any of them to waste time rescuing a mere cat.

Jeremy fell on the floor and began to drum his heels. Mrs. Oakes began to cry. "Oh, Miss Brown," she sobbed. "He will do himself a mischief."

Harriet looked about her desperately and then, in the dark shadows of the coffee room, she saw the figure of a man lying on a settle.

She walked over and looked down at him.

He was fast asleep, his hat tilted over his eyes, his gleaming Hessian boots crossed at the ankles. His dress was tailored to perfection and his cravat like sculptured snow. Normally, Harriet might have felt a little intimidated before such an indolent Exquisite, but she noted from his clothes that he was a gentleman and gentlemen were supposed to be knight errants.

6

She put her hand on his shoulder and gave it a gentle shake.

His heavy eyelids raised and a pair of eyes as green as those of a cat looked sleepily up at her.

"Sir," said Harriet, "there is a cat trapped high up in a tree. This child"—she indicated the screaming Jeremy—"is getting himself into a passion of worry and fright. Can you help?"

He swung his long legs down from the settle and stood up and swept off his hat. "Marsham," he said. "Lord Charles Marsham, at your service, ma'am."

"And I am Miss Harriet Brown, How d'ye do," said Harriet, holding out her hand.

To her embarrassment, he lifted her hand to his lips and smiled down at her. He would have been a very handsome man had not his face been marred by a sleepy, dissipated look. His voice was light and drawling.

Harriet looked at him doubtfully. This Fribble could surely hardly climb onto a stool, let alone up a pine tree.

"My lord, on second thoughts, perhaps the child should not be indulged. It is only a cat."

"Lead the way, Miss Brown. Won't do any harm to look at the creature."

Harriet walked out of the inn, followed by Lord Charles and a strangely silent Jeremy. Harriet did not know that in passing Lord Charles had hauled Jeremy to his feet and cuffed him smartly around the ears.

Lord Charles stood under the pine tree. He pushed his curly brimmed beaver back on his golden curls and looked up. Then he winced and clutched his head.

"Port," he said weakly. "Too much, demme."

"Please do not trouble yourself," pleaded Harriet.

"Not at all, Miss Brown. If you will be so good as to hold my hat and coat and look after my boots." He took off his coat and brushed it down with his hand in a finicky, absorbed way that aroused Harriet's contempt. Then he sat down on a mounting block and tenderly pulled off his boots. "Do be sure you do not get fingerprints all over them," he said. "Just leave them on the ground." He balanced his hat on top of them. Then, after what seemed a long and silent deliberation, he removed his wristbands and waistcoat and handed those to Harriet as well.

He walked to the tree and began to climb. Harriet watched in awe. He moved up the tree slowly and easily. Jeremy stood silently, holding on to a fold of her skirt.

One by one the passengers joined Harriet, and then the inn servants. Soon bets were being laid as to whether he could make it or not.

Lord Charles finally reached the cat. It was an ill-favoured-looking striped tabby with eyes as green as his own. It looked half-starved.

He seized it by the scruff of the neck and calmly began his descent, one-handed, gripping the thin trunk of the tree with his legs.

He ignored the noisy cheering as he reached the ground. He handed the cat to Harriet and looked dismally down at the wreck of his pantaloons.

"My best pair," he said sadly.

"Thank you, my lord." Harriet held out the cat to him. "We must be on our way."

"I don't want the cat," said Lord Charles. "Take the damn thing away and drown it."

"My lord, you have done a noble deed. Do not spoil it with indifference and profane language," said Miss Harriet Brown severely. She put the cat on the ground and marched off to the coach. The other passengers followed her.

Jeremy, like all spoilt brats, having successfully caused

a fuss and put everyone to a great deal of trouble, fell happily asleep.

The coach lurched and then gathered speed. The last glimpse Harriet had of Lord Charles Marsham was of him standing holding his coat and looking at the cat. He appeared to be lecturing it.

He was.

"You are a prime bit of flea-ridden trouble, demned if you ain't," said Lord Charles severely.

The shabby cat miaowed plaintively.

Lord Charles put on his boots and picked up his clothes and made his way back to the inn. The cat followed him. He went into the coffee room and called for a pot of black coffee, muttering that his head felt like the deuce.

The landlord himself came oiling forward with the coffee and cup on a tray, along with a saucer of milk and a dish of fish scraps.

"Little something for your cat, my lord," said the landlord.

"It isn't *my* cat," complained Lord Charles. The cat had leaped up onto a chair next to him and was regarding him with a steady, unwinking green gaze. "Oh, very well, feed the brute," sighed Lord Charles. "Where was that Miss Brown travelling?"

"London, my lord."

"To judge from her dress, it is hardly likely I shall meet her again. She is probably only stopping over in London before travelling on to convert the heathen and make their lives a misery. Now, I like females to be soft and pretty. Not hard-eyed reformers who make me climb trees after poxy cats. Demme, she *smelled* of churches and good works. Frightful female."

"Will you be travelling on today to London yourself, my lord?" asked the landlord.

"Yes, when I am recovered."

The landlord moved off. From the doorway, he turned and said, "I'll just find you a basket for your cat, my lord." And then he was gone.

"Odd's fish!" drawled Lord Charles Marsham. "Take you to London, you mangy brute! How would you like to see the bottom of the Thames with a stone tied around your neck, hey?"

The cat jumped on his lap, kneaded its claws into the ruin of his trousers, and began to purr.

While Harriet was reaching the last stage of her journey to London, Amy and Effy Tribble were taking tea at their friend Mrs. Marriot's with several other ladies who were hopeful of securing husbands for their daughters or relatives at the Little Season.

"Bit thin on the ground, ain't it?" said Amy Tribble as the ladies passed a list of eligibles from hand to hand. She and her twin sister Effy hoped for another triumph. Although it was they who had arranged the elopement for the Duke of Berham and Maria Kendall, society did not believe them. Mrs. Marriot's eyes sparkled with excitement. "You have not heard my news," she said. "There is one gentleman not listed. Very eligible."

"Who is he?" demanded a chorus of voices, and pencils were posed over pads of paper.

"Lord Charles Marsham, younger son of the Duke of Hambleshire."

The pencils remained poised. "It is fine that he is a duke's son," pointed out Effy Tribble, "but younger sons do not have much of the ready and our new charge has only a small dowry."

"Ah, but that's the point," said Mrs. Marriot eagerly.

"He *is* rich. Very. He is a friend of Rothschild and he took his prize money from the Peninsular Wars and invested it on the Stock Exchange very cleverly, for you see Rothschild tipped him off about the outcome of the Battle of Waterloo. Everyone else thought the Duke of Wellington had lost and they were selling stock like anything and it's my belief Rothschild cleverly spread the rumour of a defeat while having his own messenger right on the battlefield so he would know the outcome before anyone else."

"And why was this Lord Charles not on the battlefield himself?" demanded Amy.

"He was grievously ill after . . . oh, one of those battles. He had a sabre thrust right through him and everyone thought he would die. But 'tis said the great Duke of Wellington himself declared that Marsham had more lives than a cat, and so it was proved, for he rallied amazingly. He has been visiting his father in Yorkshire and is returning to London very shortly."

"Is he old?" asked Effy.

"In his thirties, but very handsome."

"And why have we not seen him before?" demanded a small, plump matron who was fretting over the fact that her daughter had not "taken" during the last Season.

"He was recovering from his wound, then he was busy making money, and then he seemed hell-bent on killing himself with dissipation, which meant if he was not riding in some race fit to break his neck, he was drinking himself nigh to death with a lot of villains in Tothill Fields."

Amy Tribble sighed and closed her notebook without bothering to write down Lord Charles's name.

"Don't like the sound of him," she said roundly.

"Oh, but he is the best catch there is," said Mrs. Marriot. "Is your new charge beautiful?"

"Doubt it," said Amy gloomily. "Daughter of a Methody. Long in the tooth. Twenty-five, I gather."

"Well," said the plump matron with a malicious giggle, "it will be pleasant to see the pair of you take a back seat while one of us gets the chance to snatch the prize."

"Sometimes I wonder about the morality of what we're doing," said Amy Tribble to her sister, Effy, as their carriage later bore them towards the City to meet Harriet, who was arriving on the mail coach. "There they all were, describing some rake as the catch of the Season. A man in his thirties and not married, hardened by wars and dissipation and no doubt riddled with the pox."

"Amy!"

"Stands to reason. If he's been with whores, he's got whores' disease."

"Amy, may I remind you it is a minister's daughter we are to refine? Mrs. Marriot did not talk about whores."

"Any man who drinks blue ruin in Tothill Fields has been with whores," said Amy with gloomy satisfaction. "Can't hope for much success with this one. Let's see what she looks like."

Harriet was pleasantly surprised when she met the Tribbles. They were disappointed in her. Her chin was too strong, her mouth too generous, and her gaze too direct.

Harriet thought Effy Tribble, with her delicate features, cloud of silver hair, and pretty clothes, a very dainty lady indeed, and tall Amy, with her sad horselike face, a plain but respectable spinster.

Both sisters forbore from commenting on Harriet's dress. There would be time enough to persuade her that half mourning was suitable enough and there was no reason to go around dressed in black.

Amy pointed out various sights as the carriage rattled along. Harriet shrank back a little. The noise was tremendous. Hawkers were calling their wares, drivers were fighting with drivers as they tried to manoeuvre their coaches through the press. A thin fog was veiling the streets. London was hardly ever free from fog in the autumn and winter months, said Amy. That, thought Harriet, must account for the unnatural pallor of the faces of the people in the streets. Even the children of the poor in Scarborough had rosy cheeks.

The bustle and roar and noise of London pressed in on her, making her feel small and lost and homesick. Neither Effy Tribble nor Amy seemed to be brands to be saved from the burning. Both looked eminently respectable. So, as she could not escape her dismal thoughts by concentrating on possible good works, Harriet reflected instead on the fashionable man who had rescued the cat. Now there was the sort of man she would never dream of marrying, although she sensibly told herself that she was the sort of female who could never in a hundred years attract such an Exquisite. And yet, he had climbed that tree so easily. And he could not surely be so very bad to go to such an effort for a mere cat. Thinking about Lord Charles effectively lifted Harriet's gloom. Why be afraid of London society when the Tribbles had proved to be sensible and kind women? And if such a fop as Lord Charles Marsham could put off his selfish, dissipated indolence to rescue a cat, then it followed that people here were like people in Scarborough, decent and honest.

They arrived at Holles Street, where Harriet was shown up to a pleasant bedroom. Maids unpacked her trunk and the Tribbles' lady's maid, Baxter, called to say she would dress her hair in a new style on the following day. There were flowers in vases and new novels on a table by the bed. A fire crackled on the hearth. A footman brought in tea and biscuits and informed Miss Brown she was to rest and then join the Misses Tribble in the drawing-room before dinner.

Left alone at last, Harriet gave way to weakness and broke down and cried. Never before had anyone thought of her comfort in any way. Her father had expected her to clean the house and make the meals and do the shopping and help in the parish work because that was her duty as his daughter and her role as a mere female. Although she did not yet know it, because of his severe, unbending morality, the Browns' visits to the parishioners were tolerated rather than welcomed. No one considered Harriet had a hard time of it. Severe Methodists were expected to enjoy a certain amount of martyrdom.

At last Harriet knelt down and prayed for God to bless the Tribbles. They were being paid to look after her, yes, but they did not need to be kind, that much she knew. For all these little thoughtful acts of kindness, she would find some way to repay them.

Baxter returned to help her dress for dinner, choosing, after much head shaking, a plain grey silk dress with black velvet bands that Harriet had bought second-hand. She dressed Harriet's hair simply, saying that perhaps, as she had so much hair, a professional hairdresser should be summoned to cut a little of it.

Harriet was not used to dealing with servants. A scrubbing woman had come in to do the heavier chores at home once a week and the rest she had done herself. So she treated Baxter and the rest of the servants with unsophisticated gratitude that went right to their hearts. Had her father been with her, uttering his usual stern proverbs, then Harriet would have been treated with cold disdain. Unlike her father, she had a genuine belief in the goodness of people, and so the servants behaved their best towards this shabby young lady and did not despise her for her clothes or for her lack of sophistication.

As the butler, Harris, said in the servants' hall later, it was a vast pity Miss Brown had to be "refined"; in his opinion, she was much better off the way she was.

When Harriet went down to the drawing-room, she was surprised to find two gentlemen present along with Effy and Amy. One, tall and thin and slightly old-fashioned in his dress, was introduced as Mr. Haddon, and a smaller man, fashionably if almost foppishly attired, as Mr. Randolph.

Harriet curtsied to both and then turned and thanked the sisters for all their kindness. Amy flushed and said gruffly it was nothing, and Effy smiled and patted Harriet's hand and said she would need to have a good night's sleep, for her lessons would begin in the morning.

"We have been studying lists of eligibles for you, Miss Brown," said Effy over dinner. "London is quite thin of suitable men. The prize would appear to be one Lord Charles Marsham, but we have decided he is not for you."

Harriet looked surprised. "I met Lord Charles on my road south," she said. "He is an elegant and lethargic gentleman who nonetheless climbed a tree at my request to rescue a cat."

Pressed for details, she told the whole story while Effy looked at Amy in a speculative way and Amy's eyelid drooped in a wink.

"I think it is rather sad, this marriage business," said Mr. Haddon.

Harriet sensed a certain sudden rigidity in Amy Tribble and then saw that her sister was looking at her with a tinge of malice in her eyes.

"How so?" demanded Amy.

"Young ladies are brought to London under the horrendous pressure of having to marry," said Mr. Haddon. "If they do not find husbands, they are made to feel like failures and no doubt have to listen to lectures on how much money has been wasted. If they do not 'take,' they are often shipped off to India, where the competition is not so strong, in the hope of catching the eye of some homesick soldier or member of the East India Company. I myself was constantly being besieged in my younger days in India by matchmaking mothers."

"I too," said Mr. Randolph with a smile. "But we are both such hardened bachelors that all their wiles were to no avail."

Now there was tension emanating from Effy Tribble. "I suppose all females want to get married some time or another," said Amy gruffly.

Mr. Haddon leaned back in his chair and examined the colour of the wine in his glass. "I think in most cases they are driven by ambitious parents and by financial necessity. Now, both you ladies have found a way of making an income, and I admire you for it. No weakness there. No longing for a strong shoulder."

Harriet sensed, rather than saw, that the Tribble sisters were very angry indeed. Effy's colour was high and her voice rather shrill as she quite deliberately changed the subject.

"Did you go to assemblies in Scarborough, Miss Brown?"

"No, ma'am," said Harriet. "My life was taken up with working for the poor and helping my father in his duties. My father believed dancing to be sinful."

"It's an enjoyable exercise," said Amy, "and I am sure the Good Lord did not put on us this earth to be miserable. How is your knowledge of music?"

"I know many hymns. Papa used to say—"

"I should not really worry about what your father used to say," said Effy gently. "The views of a Methodist minister are not suitable views for London society. You are going to be trained to be a fashionable young lady, and there is nothing sinful about that."

"Although I sometimes wonder . . ." began Mr. Haddon, but then broke off with a yelp of pain as Amy kicked him viciously under the table.

After dinner, the gentlemen and the Tribbles played whist while Harriet was told to sit by the fire and study her list of educational duties.

It was a heavy schedule: dancing master and Italian teacher in the morning, water-colour artist and deportment and manners taught by the Tribbles in the afternoon, "calls permitting." Harriet was not daunted, only relieved that her days were not going to be idle. Her eyes strayed from the page to where the sisters sat, heads bent over their cards. Amy's eyes were shiny with unshed tears.

Harriet suddenly thought, Good heavens! Of course! They are old, but they still hope to marry, and they would like to shake some sense into the gentlemen's heads.

She remembered an elderly widow, a Mrs. Butterfield, who lived in Scarborough. She had an elderly widower friend who came to call. It was obvious to Harriet that Mrs. Butterfield hoped for marriage but that the gentleman was unaware of it. Taking her courage in both hands, Harriet had pointed out to the gentleman the benefits of marriage. And so Mrs. Butterfield was happily married. Not that either of the pair had given Harriet any credit, she thought with a sigh, not knowing her father had disapproved of the match and tried to interfere, which was why Mrs. Butterfield had become unfriendly towards her. But one should always do a good deed without any hope of thanks. Rather than risk any embarrassment, Harriet decided to study the gentlemen and decide what, in this case, would be the best approach.

Later that evening, unaware that their new charge was already dreaming up matchmaking plans for *them*, Amy and Effy discussed Harriet's prospects.

"Such a good girl," said Effy.

"Not a girl," pointed out Amy. "Twenty-five is old enough for a matron. What think you of her meeting with Marsham?"

"Interesting that he should go to such an effort to please her," replied Effy. "Perhaps when he comes to London, we should send him a card and give him an opportunity to further his acquaintance. I have told Baxter to make sure Harriet puts cream on her hands and sleeps in cotton gloves. They are quite red, and the nails are too short." Effy looked complacently at her own long and polished nails.

"At first I was disappointed in her," said Amy. "Now I begin to see a lot of possibilities. Her hair is magnificent and her eyes very fine and her figure is good. Damn Yvette. Why did she have to leave us?"

Yvette, a French dressmaker, had been until recently the Tribbles' private property, living in Holles Street and designing gowns and mantles and bonnets for the sisters and their charges, which were the envy of the ton. Now Yvette had her own workshop and salon, having gone into business for herself. The sisters not only missed Yvette's skill but Yvette herself and her illegitimate baby, George, a chubby, happy creature who had brought life into the house.

"We'd better send for Yvette and get her started on Harriet right away," said Effy. "No need to go into full mourning. Black does not become her. Nor do I see her in pastels. She is old enough to wear something a bit more vivid. Such pretty gratitude! I declare I was quite moved."

"We'll do the best for her," said Amy. "There should be no trouble in schooling her. Intelligent creature."

But by the end of the following day the sisters were plunged into gloom. Harriet could read Latin and Greek classics in the original and had a surprisingly unfeminine knowledge of mathematics and science. But her singing voice proved her to be tone-deaf, and she could not learn to dance; her attempts were clumsy and wooden. The French dancing master was bewildered. Perhaps, he suggested tactfully, it was not that "mees" lacked the aptitude, it was simply that he believed people in the north of England were addicted to leaping about in wooden clogs. Nor did her drawing and water-colour painting fare any better. She had no idea of perspective and her sky did not meet the ground but stayed stuck at the top of the picture, the way a child draws it.

The sisters took over from the hired teachers in the afternoon and began to initiate Harriet into the mysteries of all the dos and don'ts of society etiquette. Never let your back touch the back of the chair. Never look round before you sit down. A footman should always be there to provide a chair. Never open a door yourself. Never sit down on a chair still warm from a gentleman's bottom. Never use your hands to do anything a servant can do for you. Always remember to cut a tiny piece of everything on your plate and put it all on your fork at once. Never offer your whole hand to a social inferior in shaking hands. An offer of one or two fingers is enough. Never curtsy to an inferior. A nod of the head will suffice. Never give a full court curtsy to a social equal. Court curtsies are reserved for royalty or royal dukes. Of course, it was quite correct to drop a full curtsy when one was being sarcastic and trying to drive home the point that although the recipient of the curtsy was one's social equal, one still despised them and thought them inferior. Never carry a fan by the handle, but always by the end when closed, pinched between the fingers. In receiving an overwarm compliment, look flustered and distressed in a maidenly way if the compliment comes from a young man. If from an old man, appear to be deaf.

Never discuss politics or religion or the poor. Read the gossip columns and listen carefully to the other ladies' gossip and pass it on. Gentlemen like to be consulted on points of dress and would rather advise a lady on the best place to buy gloves than to listen to her boring on about politics. Above all, learn to listen with grave admiration at all times. Women are stupid and weak-headed. (No, dear, we know they are not, but that is the way of the world.)

Do not, when trying to entrap some gentleman, be obvious. Finesse is the thing. The lowered eyelashes, the slight blush, the graceful movement of the arms and the pliant movement of the body. Attitudes were a very useful accomplishment and showed off the figure.

"What are Attitudes?" asked Harriet, bewildered by this flow of advice. "I have read in the papers, you know, that Miss So-and-so struck some very fine Attitudes, and it always made it sound as if she had flown into a passion."

"No, no," said Amy. "An Attitude can be anything so long as it is classical or vaguely so. Let me see if I can strike an Attitude for you."

She suddenly balanced on one great flat foot and lifted her other leg up at the back, shielded her eyes with her hand and glared into the middle distance.

Something happened inside Harriet. She could feel laughter bubbling up inside and bit her lips to stop it escaping and ended up letting out a great snort.

"Ridiculous, ain't it?" said Amy with a grin. "But take a guess. Who am I?"

"I r-really d-don't know," giggled Harriet.

"I'm Penelope awaiting the return of Odysseus," said Amy. "Or you could be a nymph startled by whoever. Nymphs were always getting startled by someone or other." She suddenly stood stock-still, her eyes rolling wildly, one shoulder up and both arms out to the side as if to ward off an attacker.

Harriet gave up trying to control herself and laughed until the tears rolled down her face. "I could never bring myself to do anything like that," she said when she had recovered.

"It is not very important," said Effy. "But you must never laugh like that in company, my dear. Do not show any excess of emotion. Gentle tears coursing down the cheeks are all very well and show a nice sensibility. But never roar or bawl. Now put those books over on that table on your head and learn to walk up and down, curtsy, and sit down without letting them fall."

Both sisters watched with approval as Harriet carried out the instructions with stately elegance.

"Bless me, very good," said Amy. "Why is it you cannot learn to dance, I wonder? Effy, go and play a waltz. Now, pretend I am the man, Harriet. No, do not look down. And one and two . . . Not bad, not bad at all. What ails that dancing master?"

Harriet blushed. "I am not used to having a man's hand at my waist."

"Odso? Then you had better get used to it." Amy rang the bell. When Harris answered the summons, she commanded the startled butler to waltz. Harriet stumbled and moved like a wooden doll. "Keep at it," admonished Amy.

Effy played on. Then Harris' place was taken by the first footman, then the second, and finally by Mr. Haddon, who came to call. Out of breath, Harriet pleaded for a rest and then said, "Why do you and Mr. Haddon not show me how it is done, Miss Amy? The waltz, I mean."

Harriet sat down and watched with satisfaction as the normally ungainly Amy drifted around the drawing-room in Mr. Haddon's arms, until Effy hit a nasty chord and slammed down the piano lid, saying pettishly she could not play anymore.

Chapter 2

*. . . don't girls like a rake better than a
milksop?*

—*Thackeray*

LORD CHARLES MARSHAM HAD
an elegant mansion in Green Street.
His staff were well-trained and content with their jobs, as
Lord Charles preferred to keep his roistering away from
home. Three weeks had passed since he had rescued that
cat and somehow it was still with him—and more de-
manding than a wife, he often thought sourly. It followed
him everywhere like a shadow and refused to be confined
to the kitchens.

His friend Jack Perkins, a former colonel, was sprawled
in Lord Charles's library, glaring awfully at the cat, which
had attempted to scratch him. Jack had tried to retaliate

by kicking it and had been prevented from doing so by Lord Charles.

"It is only a cat, demme," drawled Lord Charles weakly. "I have the devil of a headache and I cannot bear you shouting and stomping like an avenging fury. What are we doing today?"

Jack was usually the instigator of every wild episode in Lord Charles's life, Lord Charles being too indolent to think up any of his own. Their mutual friends privately considered Jack Perkins a bad influence.

"You've forgotten already," accused Jack. "Slap-bang-up Cyprian party at the Argyle Rooms tonight."

Lord Charles, who had just risen from his bed, although it was three in the afternoon, wrapped his dressing-gown a little closer about his body and shuddered. "Whores were never to my taste, Jack, and that you know. Gambling, racing, boxing, yes. Tarts, no."

"There are to be some of the highest-flyers in London there," said Jack. "You can't continue to live like a monk. When did you last look at a female?"

"I forget," sighed Lord Charles. "Salamanca, was it? Small, dainty thing with big dark eyes. No, Jack, I don't think I shall go this evening."

Jack Perkins thought quickly. If Lord Charles did not go, he would have to endure his own company—he did not consider women, whores or otherwise, company—and that he could not bear. He was not popular with his own sex, a fact that seemed to have escaped the indolent lord opposite.

The bond that held Lord Charles to Jack Perkins was that he believed Jack had saved his life when he had received that sabre wound, by carrying him on his back all the way back from the front lines. Jack let him continue to believe it, but a lowly foot-soldier had borne Lord Charles to safety, before returning to the battle, where he had been subsequently shot. Jack had been beside Lord Charles's bed when he regained consciousness. Before he fainted from the pain of his wound and loss of blood, Lord Charles had been dimly aware of being lifted and carried. He assumed Jack had done it and thanked him, and Jack had gracefully accepted his thanks, hoping all the while that the real rescuer would never materialize to take the credit away from him.

Jack Perkins was tall and broad-shouldered, with large liquid brown eyes in a rather brutal face that was fiery-red due to the amount he drank. Unlike Lord Charles, he did not exercise or occasionally retreat from dissipation to cure the harm done by long nights of carousing.

"Tell you what," he said, "we'll only stay for a short while and then go on to Watier's and gamble the night away."

This was more to Lord Charles's taste. He rarely lost.

He rose wearily to his feet and stretched and yawned. "I had better dress," he said, "and take the air."

He sauntered from the room and closed the door behind him. Jack smiled evilly on the cat, which had tried to follow its master, but now found itself shut inside. Jack rose and made a dive for the cat, which darted away from him and then let out a piercing, wailing, demented cry for help.

Lord Charles had stopped on the stairs to talk to his butler. He heard the cat, and with surprising speed in one so normally lazy and indolent, he darted back to the library and flung open the door. The cat leaped straight up into his arms.

He stroked the cat's fur and said in his lazy voice, "I

should have explained, dear Jack, that I am quite capable of killing anyone who harms this animal. Do I make myself clear?"

His eyes were hard and cold. Jack shifted uneasily and gave an awkward laugh. "Just having a bit of fun with the kitty," he said.

But the expression in Lord Charles's eyes did not change. "I am warning you, Jack," he said, "leave this cat alone in future."

He turned to leave. The cat hung its head over his shoulder and glared at Jack, its green eyes seeming to hold the same cold warning and menace Jack had just seen in its master's. Although neither a Catholic, nor a particularly religious man, Jack was, nonetheless, highly superstitious and still believed in witches. He crossed himself as the library door closed again.

Harriet had been out on her first social call, a sedate evening of gossip with the ladies at Mrs. Marriot's, and escorted by Amy Tribble, Effy having complained of the headache while secretly hoping that Mr. Haddon and Mr. Randolph would call while Amy was gone. Effy often dreamt of working both gentlemen up to the point of proposing, and then refusing one of them and saying magnanimously, 'Take my sister instead.' But which should she refuse? Mr. Randolph was agreeable and interested in all the things Effy was interested in herself, such as the latest gossip and the latest novels. Mr. Haddon could be severe. But Amy was interested in Mr. Haddon, and that lent him added lustre in Effy's eyes. The twin sisters had been rivals for years.

Harriet was wearing one of the new gowns that had quickly been designed for her by Yvette and then made by Yvette's team of seamstresses. It was of striped lilac-and-grey sarsenet, meant to be half mourning, but looking, Harriet thought uneasily,· very French and, yes, somehow naughty with its low square neckline. Their carriage slowed and then stopped in a press of traffic outside the Argyle Rooms. People were arriving, people were leaving. Harriet looked with interest. The ladies were surprisingly immodest, she thought, very free in their manners, laughing and chattering.

"Cyprians," said Amy shortly. "Whores. Must be a party. Not for your eyes, Harriet. A lady does not know such things exist."

But Harriet continued to look. "Are all these men unmarried?" she asked.

"Of course not," replied Amy.

"Then what are they doing with these women?"

"Oh, Harriet, for pity's sake, what do you think they are doing?"

"But if they have wives . . . ?"

"Marriage in society is mostly a business contract. You find your fun *after* marriage." Amy went on to soften the blow by describing how all *their* previous charges had married for love, until she realized Harriet was not listening. The girl was staring fixedly at a handsome, dissipated-looking man who was standing on the steps waiting for his carriage. Two prostitutes came out and flung their arms about his neck and he smiled down on them and shook his head and then kissed each one heartily.

"Haven't seen him before," said Amy, leaning forward to see what was holding Harriet's attention. "Wonder who he is?"

"That is Lord Charles Marsham," said Harriet calmly.

"Oh." Amy's face fell. She would need to tell Effy there

was no hope there. Not that she blamed him for frequenting a Cyprian party. Men did those sorts of things, and genteel ladies pretended not to know about them. But he looked so very handsome and yet so very decadent that Amy knew he would never be interested in anyone as good and honest as Harriet Brown. And then it seemed as if he had recognized Harriet, for his gaze suddenly sharpened.

Lord Charles studied their carriage until the traffic shifted and they moved on and it was lost to view.

Could that possibly be the girl who had asked him to rescue the cat? He was sure there could not be another woman in London with those vivid blue eyes, black hair, and that square jawline. Jack Perkins came out behind him. "Hey, friend," he said, "come back in."

"Going to walk," said Lord Charles suddenly and headed off rapidly down the street. The traffic was still moving slowly and he recognized the rented livery carriage after walking only a few hundred yards. Not knowing quite why he was so interested, he followed the carriage on foot, keeping always behind it.

It finally drew to a halt outside a house in Holles Street. The flickering light of the whale-oil lamp over the door shone on a brass plate with the name "Tribble" inscribed on it in curly letters, dating from the time when London did not have street numbers. The two ladies got out. One was tall and mannish and quite old; the other, he was sure, was that girl—what was her name? Harriet, that was it, Harriet Brown.

He strode forward and swept them a bow. "We meet again, Miss Brown," he said, while his expert eye noticed with surprise the sophistication of her gown.

Her steady eyes regarded him with compassion. Harriet had decided to be sorry for this sinful creature. She introduced him to Amy.

"Saw you on the steps of the Argyle Rooms," said Amy bluntly. "Did you follow us here?"

"Yes."

"Why?"

Lord Charles looked amused. "I recognized Miss Brown and decided it would only be polite to call on her and tell her about the welfare of the cat."

"Midnight ain't the time for calls," said Amy testily.

But Harriet stepped forward. "You still have the cat? Oh, how very good of you. Is it well?"

"Extremely well, Miss Brown, and sends you its regards."

"Is it male or female?"

"Male, Miss Brown."

"And what do you call it?"

"I have not given it a name." Lord Charles had a sudden fit of inspiration. "I think *you* should choose a name for it, Miss Brown, and I shall call on you tomorrow to learn your choice."

"I thank you, my lord," said Amy firmly, "but tomorrow is not suitable. Come, Harriet."

But the minister's daughter stood her ground. If Lord Charles had indeed kept the cat, then Lord Charles was not all bad and there was hope of reform. It was her duty to help the wicked see the light.

"I am sure, Miss Tribble," she said firmly, "that you will find I have ten minutes to spare at three o'clock in the afternoon and would be most glad to see Lord Charles."

While Amy stood dumbfounded, Lord Charles swept off his hat again and bowed and took his leave.

"You great ninny," said Amy as soon as they were indoors. "You are supposed to be in training to find a suitable husband, not to encourage the doubtful attentions of a womanizer."

"There is hope there for reform," said Harriet. "That cat may be the making of him."

"Pah!" said Miss Amy Tribble.

It was fortunately highly fashionable for gentlemen to carry muffs. Lord Charles therefore popped the cat inside a large sable one after he had dressed with his usual care and set out for the Tribbles on the following day. To his slight annoyance, he nearly bumped into Jack Perkins, who was coming to call on him.

"Where are you bound?" asked Jack curiously.

"Making a call on a lady," said Lord Charles laconically.

He put the cat-filled muff on the seat of his curricle and then jumped in beside it and picked up the reins.

"Which one is it?" asked Jack eagerly. "Must be one of the high-flyers for you to be making an afternoon call. Harriet Wilson? One of her sisters?"

"No, not a whore," said Lord Charles. "Stand away, there's a good chap, or you will make me late."

Jack would have persisted, leaning on the edge of the carriage, had not he suddenly noticed that the muff appeared to have developed a pair of eyes that were watching him steadily. He gave an exclamation and jumped back. Lord Charles smiled at him and his carriage moved off.

Jack Perkins stood on the pavement, looking bewildered. It must have been a trick of the light. Then he realized that a Lord Charles who was going to call on a lady might be a Lord Charles who was contemplating marriage, and that did not suit Jack at all. Although he would not admit it to himself, part of his brain was dimly aware that a lot of society doors would be closed to him without Lord Charles's friendship. He decided he must wait to find out the name of this lady and then do his best to drive a wedge between the pair.

Lord Charles was bowling along Oxford Street when he saw an old army friend, Guy Sutherland. He reined in his horses and called down, "Just arrived in town?"

"No, been here a few weeks," said Guy lazily. He was a large, formless sort of man with amiable, childlike eyes. "Coming to the club?"

"I am making calls. I am going to the Tribbles in Holles Street."

"You're too young to have a daughter of marriageable age," said Guy.

"And not married either," rejoined Lord Charles. "Why should I have a daughter?"

"It's them Tribbles. That's their business. They bring out girls who are a problem to their parents."

"Odso! Tell me more."

"Odd couple of eccentrics. Twins. Ought to be in their winding sheets by now. They've made a success of marrying off females. Advertise in *The Morning Post.* Charge a high amount, from all reports."

"Do you happen to know if a Miss Harriet Brown is their latest?"

"Never heard of her. But rumour has it they've got a new victim."

"Let us meet later," said Lord Charles. "At White's, say about five?"

"Gladly. You can tell me all about the fabulous Tribbles. I say, you ain't still got that fellow Perkins in tow?"

"He is in Town, yes."

"Well, leave him behind when you come to White's, there's a good chap. Never could abide the fellow."

Lord Charles smiled pleasantly, but there was an edge

in his voice as he said, "Jack Perkins is a good friend of mine and I will not discuss him."

"As you will," said Guy mildly. "Still, I'd rather see you on your own." And, with an indolent wave of one massive arm, he strolled off, and Lord Charles continued on his way to Holles Street.

Now what had brought Harriet Brown to the Tribbles? mused Lord Charles. Perhaps she was not their charge but a hired companion or governess. But her clothes the evening before had been expensively cut. And why was he going out of his way to call on such a correct and dull female?

He had come this far, better get it over with.

He rolled to a stop in front of the Tribbles' house in Holles Street and sat for a few moments, reluctant to go in. He was aware of his worth on the marriage market. If Miss Brown was being brought out by the Tribbles, would he not be raising false hopes by his call? A chill wind blew down the street and he shivered. He called to his tiger to go to the horses' heads and climbed down, holding the cat in the large muff.

The door was answered by Harris, the butler. He departed with Lord Charles's card and returned after some time to say Miss Effy Tribble was in the drawing-room and would be pleased to receive him.

Lord Charles mounted the stairs behind the butler and then was ushered into the drawing-room. Effy rose to meet him. Despite Amy's forebodings about Lord Charles, Effy had begun to entertain high hopes of him after hearing of how he had pursued their carriage the evening before. But when she looked up at the tall Exquisite with the lazy green eyes and thin, white, dissipated face, her heart sank. Never had a man been more unsuitable for such a strict young lady as Harriet Brown.

But none of this showed on Effy's face as she begged him to be seated and rang for cakes and wine. Lord Charles looked about him with pleasure. The room was a comfortable mixture of different pieces of furniture, flowers in vases, pretty pictures, a work-basket with silk threads spilling out of it, and the latest books and magazines. The fire crackled cheerfully behind its fender of Britannia metal and the air was delicately scented. He felt oddly at home. Effy Tribble was a charming lady with her cloud of silver hair under a lacy cap and her trim figure in a blue velvet gown.

"Will you not let Harris take your muff, my lord?" said Effy.

"No, ma'am, I've got the cat in it."

"The cat!"

"It's a scruffy cat which Miss Brown asked me to rescue from a tree on her road south. I thought she might like to see it."

"Of course," said Effy weakly. She rang the bell again and when a footman answered its summons, she told the footman to go and see what was keeping Miss Amy and Miss Brown.

What was keeping Miss Amy and Miss Brown was a massive row. Amy wanted Harriet to wear one of her new gowns. Harriet wanted to wear one of her old ones, pointing out that going to any unnecessary fuss might make Lord Charles think she was interested in him, and that she most certainly was not. Amy blustered and swore, and Harriet then proceeded to give her a lecture on the disgusting use of profanity. At last Amy realized that Harriet meant to sit there all day until she got what she wanted, and so allowed her to wear a gown that Amy told her was the colour of slurry and just about as interesting. It had a cotton lace collar and cuffs—cotton lace! thought Amy with a shudder—and the waistline was old-fashioned, being at the waist instead of up under the armpits. Harriet had had this gown for quite some years and it was a trifle short and showed her ankles. There was surely nothing much she could do to spoil the glory of her hair, thought Amy, until Harriet swept it up on top of her head in a hard knot.

Lord Charles rose as Harriet and Amy entered the drawing-room, and made a magnificent bow.

Harriet curtsied beautifully, the sisters noticed, trying to gain comfort from little things to make up for the awful spectacle Harriet was making of herself in that gown.

They would have been relieved had they known that Harriet was deeply regretting wearing such an old dress. Lord Charles's appearance was so exquisite that she felt dowdy and intimidated. His green eyes flicked a glance at her ankles and she coloured slightly and ineffectually tried to pull her skirt down to conceal them.

"So this, Miss Brown," said Lord Charles when they were all seated, "is the cat." He fished in his muff and brought out the cat.

All these green eyes, thought Amy. It's like being in the jungle. Lord Charles's eyes were grass-green, and the cat looked from one to the other with an unblinking green stare.

It settled itself down on Lord Charles's lap, yawned delicately, closed its eyes and went to sleep.

"It seems very contented, my lord," volunteered Harriet, "and in good coat. You obviously look after it very well."

"Very well," said Harriet coldly. She had thought that affection for the stray cat showed a sign of good in Lord Charles. Now it appeared his soul was as cold and manicured as his appearance. Effy and Amy exchanged looks of dismay.

"So what will you call it?" asked Lord Charles.

"I do not believe in giving animals elaborate names," said Harriet. "I shall call it Tom. It is a tom-cat, after all."

"Are you enjoying your stay in London, Miss Brown?"

"Yes, very much. But there is so much to learn."

"Such as?"

"Oh." Harriet sighed and wrinkled her brow. "Watercolour painting and dancing and manners and etiquette and 'Don't do this and don't do that.' "

"I thought those were all things any young miss learned in her cradle."

"Not my cradle, my lord. I was brought up to do more important things."

"And what is more important?"

"Caring for the sick and poor of my father's parish, learning to read the classics in the original, studying my Bible."

And if that catalogue don't put him off, nothing will, thought Amy grimly.

"Then why do you attend such a worldly and frivolous event as the Little Season?"

"My parents are both dead," said Harriet candidly. "My father died recently and left me nigh penniless. My aunt, Lady Owen, decided to give me a small dowry and send me to London to these ladies for schooling."

"So you hope to marry?"

"Let me rather say that I am obliged to marry. I have no alternative."

"You could find work."

"I do not have the necessary qualifications to be a governess," said Harriet. "I have not had experience of running a large establishment and so I am not trained as a housekeeper."

"There are other jobs," pointed out Lord Charles.

"Yes, I could be a chambermaid or washerwoman.

35

There are very few jobs open to women. Doctors and lawyers are all men. Preachers are men. Even our stay-makers are men."

Effy let out a faint scream.

He leaned back in his chair and idly stroked the cat and studied her. "I made my money by gambling on the Stock Exchange," he said. "You say you have a small dowry. I could show you how to put that to use."

"That small dowry, my lord, is in my aunt's possession and will not be released by her or her lawyers until the marriage settlements are signed."

"So you have no assets?"

"Only myself, my lord, and that is already on the market."

This was going too far. Amy glared at Harriet. "Miss Brown," she said severely. "I do not like correcting you in front of a guest, but I must point out that your speech is too free. You will give Lord Charles a disgust of you."

"But my only interest in Lord Charles is the welfare of the cat, you know that," pointed out Harriet. "And *his* only interest in me is to get shot of the cat."

Effy let out a faint bleating noise.

"On the contrary," said Lord Charles with easy gallantry. "I came to renew my acquaintance with a lady whose face and charm of manner so attracted me on our first meeting."

Harriet's eyes lit up with amusement. "How prettily you do it," she said. "But such fustian!"

"How true," said Lord Charles with a wicked smile. "But as I shall still want to know how the cat fares, I shall beg permission to take you driving on the morrow."

"I don't . . ." began Amy but fell silent as Harriet held up one hand.

"Let me think," Harriet said severely.

Her eyes assessed Lord Charles and Lord Charles smiled sweetly at her and wondered what on earth she was thinking.

Harriet was turning over in her mind the problem of how best to help the Tribbles with their love life. Lord Charles was a man, a man who went to clubs and talked to other men and who might be persuaded to drop an encouraging word in Mr. Haddon's ear, or Mr. Randolph's, for that matter. He appeared amiable enough.

"Yes, I should like that very much," said Harriet. "Shall we say three o'clock?"

"Five o'clock is the fashionable hour, Miss Brown."

"But my desire for your company is not fashionable," said Harriet.

For one mad moment, he wondered whether Miss Brown was flirting with him.

"May I hope it is a flattering interest?"

"No, you may not, my lord. I am ever practical."

"Then I look forward to tomorrow." He lifted the cat, which protested sleepily, and set it down on the floor. "Stay there, Tom," he said. "Your new home."

He rose and bowed, first to the Tribbles and then to Harriet.

He strolled down the stairs. The cat shot after him and, with a flying leap, landed on his shoulder and clung on like grim death.

Harriet leaned over the banister on the landing as Lord Charles tried to prize the cat loose.

"Tom appears very attached to you, my lord."

Lord Charles got the cat free and set it on the stair. It began to tremble and let out a pathetic wail.

He sighed and scooped it up and put it in his muff.

"I had better take it, Miss Brown," he said ruefully. "It might have a seizure."

"Which all goes to show," said Harriet triumphantly after the street door had closed behind him, "that there is good in everyone."

"I have never heard such a load of soiled garters," shouted Amy. "You sat there as cool as cucumbers, telling that Fribble you were on the market and you hadn't much money. No one will want you if you go around making speeches like that, not even a minister, particularly not a minister. And why waste time going out driving with a rake?"

"He appears very fashionable to me," said Harriet, unruffled. "It will do my consequence no harm to be seen with him."

"And," said Effy Tribble consolingly to her furious sister when they were alone, "you can't really argue with that."

Miss Spiggs and "Dr." Frank had taken up residence in a small apartment in Bloomsbury. Frank had not told Miss Spiggs he was married to Bertha, whom he had left behind in Bath. Although they were masquerading as man and wife, Frank had not even kissed Miss Spiggs or held her hand. He told her his love for her was so pure and his intentions so honourable that he had no intention of "making things warmer" until he felt free to marry her. Miss Spiggs was enjoying the feeling of appearing to be a married lady. She sat in the evenings and told Frank everything she knew about the Tribbles, although there was not much to add to Frank's knowledge, Frank already having worked for the Tribbles himself. Miss Spiggs herself had recently been employed as companion to the Tribbles' previous charge, a Miss Maria Kendall, and had lost that job and the subsequent job of companion to

Maria's mother all because of the Tribble sisters' spite—or so she persuaded herself. But together, Frank and Miss Spiggs finally arrived at the Tribbles' greatest weakness, their pride in their success. If, said Frank, they could kidnap the Tribbles' latest "client" and hold her for ransom, then the Tribbles would probably pay a large sum to get her back.

Miss Spiggs looked at him doubtfully. "I do not think, you know, that they have very much money," she said.

"But that nabob, Haddon, has," said Frank gleefully. "They'll go weeping to him and he'll pay up."

Mr. Desmond Callaghan was back in London. He, too, wished nothing but ill on the Tribbles. Although he had tricked their aunt into leaving him everything in her will and cutting out the Tribbles, that everything had proved to be nothing but debt. Convinced the Tribbles had money, he had courted Effy, only to insult her when he learned she was virtually penniless. That was when Mr. Haddon had challenged him to a duel and he had had to flee the country. He not only wished revenge on the Tribbles, whom he blamed for all his discomfort, but on that footman, Frank, who had left the Tribbles' employ to aid him, only to thieve all his valuables.

He decided to lie low for a little and study how best he could hurt the Tribbles and perhaps make a profit for himself.

Chapter 3

But I'm not so think as you drunk I am.
—*Sir John Collings Squire*

LORD CHARLES SPENT A pleasant evening with Guy Sutherland, unaware that Jack Perkins was searching for him. They left White's after an early dinner and repaired to Guy's comfortable lodgings and sat beside the fire, remembering battles and their school days at Eton.

Jack had come to regard Lord Charles as his personal property and was as jealous as any slighted woman. In fact, he blamed the mysterious lady Lord Charles had gone to see for Lord Charles's absence.

And so it was, when he called early the following day—twelve noon *was* early in London society—it was to find that his friend was engaged to take a certain lady driving.

Concealing his dismay, Jack suggested they should hail the new day with a couple of bottles of champagne. Lord Charles amiably agreed. Port followed the champagne, and then brandy. Lord Charles finally looked at the clock with fuddled eyes and remembered he had promised to take Miss Brown driving at three and he was in his altitudes and his undress.

He howled for his valet, dressed in haste, and, ignoring Jack's protests, made his way shakily to his carriage. The cat, Tom, slunk out of the house after him and leaped up on the seat. Normally Lord Charles would have shooed the cat out, but he felt so bleary, so totally drunk that he could not be bothered. He set off, driving carefully.

Neither Effy nor Amy noticed his condition, for he rallied tremendously and presented a good front. It was only when Harriet was seated beside him that he realized once more that he was infernally drunk and that the press of traffic seemed to be immense because he was seeing two of everything.

Somehow he managed to reach the Park. As soon as they were through the gates, Harriet said sharply, "Halt the carriage, my lord."

He obeyed her and then looked at her dreamily. Her face seemed to be a long way away. It was like looking at her down the wrong end of a telescope.

Harriet climbed down and commanded him to move over.

Too fuddled to protest, he did as he was bid. Harriet climbed into his vacated place and picked up the reins.

"Are you sure you can drive, Miss Brown?" he asked, quite pleased that he had managed to enunciate a whole sentence clearly.

"I think so, my lord. Please be quiet and take deep breaths."

"Why?"

"You are disgustingly drunk."

"Yes, ma'am," agreed Lord Charles meekly.

Harriet clicked her tongue at the horses and then said, "Walk on," and to her relief, they did. She had no intention of telling this boozy lord that she had never driven anything other than her father's donkey cart before. Harriet was determined not to abandon Lord Charles until he was made to see the folly of his ways. She had to help the Tribbles, and a sober Lord Charles would be a better assistant than a drunk one. Glad it was not the fashionable hour and the Park was therefore thin of company, Harriet drove sedately round and round. The cat fell asleep, its head on Lord Charles's knee, and Lord Charles fell asleep as well. Harriet drove back to the gates, stopped the carriage, opened her reticule, which was full of useful items, and took out a lead pencil and a notebook. She wrote: "Dear Misses Tribble, Do not be concerned for me. I am spending more time in the Park with Lord Charles than is fashionably correct, but we have much to talk about. H. Brown." Harriet did not have any pin money. She searched in Lord Charles's pockets until she found a shilling and then called to a passing urchin and handed the boy the shilling and the note and told him to deliver the note to Holles Street. Then, in case the Tribbles should come looking for her before she had had a chance to sober Lord Charles, she bravely drove out of the Park to look for a less fashionable spot. She decided on Kensington Gardens. She knew they lay to the west of Hyde, once more she had to stop, this time at Hyde Park toll, and search Lord Charles for money under the amused gaze of the tollkeeper. Then off again along the leafy Brompton Road. A thin flat disk of a sun was bleaching London into pale-golds and light-browns. The wind was chill and she

43

was glad she had had the foresight to put on two pet-
ticoats. Her carriage dress, designed for her by Yvette, was
of blue kerseymere, edged with fur, and worn under one
of Effy's cloaks.

She turned into Kensington Gardens, hoping always
that nothing would happen to frighten the horses, for she
knew she could not handle them if they grew in the least
frisky. Kensington Gardens had become a middle-class
venue. Few people were out on this cold day. She turned
the carriage off the walk and drove along under the trees
and came to a stop under a huge sycamore. It had a few
jutting-out lower branches and she jumped down and tied
the horses' reins to one of them. Then she returned to-the
carriage, wrapped a bearskin rug about the sleeping lord's
knees and put a fold of it over the cat, took out a small
book of essays and began to read.

After an hour, Lord Charles awoke with a start, the
sounds of battle still in his ears, for he had been dreaming
of the war. He looked about him in a dazed way and then
at his companion, who was turning the pages of her book.

"What are we doing here, ma'am?" he asked plaintively.

Harriet put down her book. "So you are awake, my
lord. It was necessary to take you somewhere where you
could sleep off your debauch in peace. You were in a
disgusting condition."

"I am sorry, Miss Brown," said Lord Charles ruefully.

"You must be aware that the taking of strong drink is
a sign of weakness, not of manhood. Strong men can face
the day without resource to alcohol."

"I now have the headache," said Lord Charles crossly,
"and you are making it worse by sitting there giving me
a jaw-me-dead. I have already apologized. Please be lady-
like enough to accept my apology."

"Very well," said Harriet. "We shall talk about your sad propensity to drink on another occasion."

Lord Charles briefly closed his eyes. There will not be another occasion if I can help it, he thought bleakly.

"The reason I wish you sober and not drunk is because I am in need of your help," said Harriet.

"Indeed?" he drawled. "Marriage, I suppose."

"Yes, but not mine. It is time Miss Effy and Miss Amy Tribble were married."

He blinked. "It is time both of 'em were dead," he pointed out.

"Nonsense. They have two friends, a Mr. Haddon and a Mr. Randolph." She took out her notebook again. "See! I will write the names down for you so that you do not forget. I wish you to seek out these gentlemen and some-how put the idea of marriage into their minds."

"I know Haddon by sight. Nabob, isn't he? Rich as Golden Ball. Put the idea of marriage in his mind, and he'll up and choose himself a pretty young widow."

"I do not think so," said Harriet primly. "Both gentle-men spend a great deal of time with the sisters. The Trib-bles should not have to worry about work at their age."

"My capable Miss Brown. If both gentlemen are such constant visitors, would it not be easier for you yourself to drop a word in their bachelor ears?"

"It is better that such an idea should come from a man," said Harriet. "All men, no matter how kind and good, have a deep contempt for women's ideas."

His head ached and Miss Brown's dictatorial manner was irritating him greatly. "Do you not think, Miss Brown," he said acidly, "that I might have more impor-tant things to do with my time than play Cupid to a couple of elderly females?"

"You have nothing more important to do with your

time," said Harriet evenly. "Frequenting Cyprians and addling your brains with drink are worthless pastimes."

Lord Charles searched his mind in an effort to bring up some worthy pastime but could not think of any. He eyed Harriet in a calculating way. He wondered what it would be like to knock Miss Brown off that self-made pedestal of hers. And then, what else had he to do? He was bored. He was growing increasingly angry with Jack Perkins, feeling he had been manipulated into getting drunk. Since his return from the wars, he had lazily gone along with what Jack wanted. Certainly, the man had saved his life, but he, Lord Charles Marsham, was weary of having noisy nights with grey days tinged with guilt to follow. He would not go so far as to seduce Miss Brown, but it would be amusing to make her fall in love with him.

He smiled into her eyes and raised her gloved hand and kissed it. Harriet hung her head and blushed. Good, thought Lord Charles. First move to me.

He is angry with me, thought Harriet, confused and sad. I do believe he plans to make me fall in love with him to teach me a lesson. Then she brightened. All she had to do was pretend to be increasingly fond of him, and while the game amused him, he might do something for the Tribbles.

She smiled up at him shyly. Her eyelashes were very long, he noticed, and that unfashionably generous mouth of hers was just made for kissing. "I shall be glad to be of help to you," said Lord Charles. "Have we not been out for some time? Will the Misses Tribble not be worried about you?"

"I sent them a note," said Harriet, "while you were asleep. I am afraid I robbed you of a shilling, and then another shilling for the toll."

"Do you not have any pin money, Capability Brown?"

46

"None at all."

"That is sad. There must be many frippery things you long to buy."

"I have no interest in fripperies," said Miss Harriet Brown sternly, but then, with a disarming smile, she added, "No, that is not precisely true. I saw a painted fan in Exeter Change. A trifling thing with a picture of an Italian scene—you know, the usual Italian scene, crag and temple and approaching thunderstorm. Not fashionable and only a shilling, but I did want it."

"You will need to have some card money for the social rounds."

"I do not play cards. I do not approve of gambling."

"Oh, Miss Brown, of what in society do you approve?"

A mischievous smile lit up her eyes. "I approve of the Tribbles."

"In other words, you are reminding me of my duty? Very well, Miss Brown. I shall seek out Mr. Haddon. Now, if you will change places with me. I shall drive you back." He jumped down and the cat rolled over and protested sleepily. "How did that thing get there?" he demanded.

"You brought it," said Harriet, getting down and walking around to the passenger side of the carriage. "Do you not remember? No, of course, you would not." And having effectively reminded Lord Charles of his drunken state, she climbed into the carriage again.

Neither Effy nor Amy had expected to have to lecture Miss Harriet Brown on her morals, but that is exactly what they did when she returned after an absence of nearly two hours. Harriet placidly agreed with every word and apologized prettily, saying she had forgotten the time. She and Lord Charles had not discussed anything very important.

Mr. Haddon and Mr. Randolph came around that evening for a game of cards and the sisters confided their worries about Harriet to the two gentlemen. "Perhaps," said Effy, "one of you could seek him out and find out if he is really such a monster of depravity as he appears to be. Sound him out about marriage."

Lord Charles, on approaching his home, recognized Jack Perkins' carriage outside. He suddenly decided he could not bear any more of his friend's company that day and drove on to his club to begin the work on Mr. Haddon and Mr. Randolph. But although both gentlemen were members, neither was to be found in the club rooms. He decided to go and see Guy Sutherland instead.

The large man gave him a warm welcome and suggested they spend the evening at the playhouse. Edmund Kean was performing in *The Merchant of Venice.* To Lord Charles's surprise, Guy really did want to listen to the play instead of ogling the prostitutes or getting drunk in the box. The performance was excellent and Lord Charles found himself wondering whether Miss Brown would enjoy it as well. She was an awful puritan, but, on the other hand, she did not seem to have much fun. As a start to winning her affections, it might be a good idea to go to Exeter Change in the morning and look for that fan. Guy did not want to go to the green-room after the play either, saying he preferred actors when they were on the stage and found them deuced tedious off it.

They went back to his lodgings and drank tea and talked about the play. At last, Lord Charles said, "I've been thinking about all those battles. How far away it all seems now. I am lucky to be alive."

"You are indeed," agreed Guy, spearing a slice of bread

on the toasting fork and holding it to the flames of the fire. "Poor little Corporal Flanagan. How he ever got you up on his back, I'll never know."

Lord Charles went very still. "Flanagan?" he asked. "What has he to do with it?"

"Heard about it afterwards from his widow. Don't you remember Bridget Flanagan, who followed her man right up to the front lines? Flanagan found you lying with that sabre wound and the little Irishman gets his missus to load you onto his back and he ran with you from the front lines. Then the poor fellow went straight back and got himself killed."

"I was under the impression that Jack Perkins saved my life," said Lord Charles in a thin voice.

"You are mistaken. Bridget Flanagan wouldn't tell a lie. Besides, Jack was alongside of me when you were being rescued. Ask him. He'll tell you."

"And where is the Widow Flanagan now?"

"In Cork, I believe. That's where Flanagan said he came from. If you want her direction, I think Captain Flaherty has it. He is at Limmer's at the moment."

"I must send her something," said Lord Charles. "Demme, I've been labouring under the impression that Jack saved my life, which is why . . ."

"Which is why you've been allowing him to manage your life and camp out in your quarters for most of the day. Bad fellow, Jack. Would have told you yesterday, but you seemed monstrous set on the man."

"Tell me, Guy, am I such a weakling, such a fool as to spend my nights looking at the bottom of several bottles or riding fit to break my neck?"

"No, no," said Guy soothingly. "War fever, that's all. Takes us all a while to settle down."

Lord Charles's temper was made worse by the knowledge on his late return home that Jack Perkins was waiting in the library.

As soon as he walked in, Jack said accusingly, "And where have you been? I have been waiting for you this age."

"You're worse than a wife, Jack," said Lord Charles. "Sit down, man. It is about time we talked about that famous rescue of yours—you know, when you carried me from the battlefield."

"I can't wait here any longer," blustered Jack, making for the door. "I have things to do."

"A moment, my friend. You let me believe you had saved my life when in fact the hero was poor little Corporal Flanagan. His captain is in Town and I am sure he will confirm the facts—that is, if you think they need any confirmation."

"I never said I'd rescued you," howled Jack.

"You most certainly let me think so. It would be a good idea if we did not see each other for some time."

"I am your friend. Your best friend. What has come between us?"

"One monstrous lie."

"You are only using that as an excuse. It's this female. Who is she?"

"There is no female. Go away, Jack, and stop enacting scenes like a jilted lover. It is distasteful."

Jack Perkins burst into tears, which did not move Lord Charles in the least, because it was highly fashionable for men to cry. Lord Charles rang the bell and said to his butler, "Show Mr. Perkins out."

Jack went out into a world that had become friendless. He refused to admit to himself that he had lied to Lord Charles, to admit that Lord Charles would not have tolerated his company for so long had he not believed in that rescue. It was all the fault of some simpering female who had got her claws into Lord Charles. Well, he would follow him and find out her name and then he would make her sorry!

That same evening saw Harriet's first introduction to cards. At first she was horrified when Amy suggested she learn to play. Gambling was sinful and had been the ruin of as many families as drink, said Harriet sternly. But Amy pointed out that the present company all enjoyed a game of cards and none of them was a hardened gambler. It was a social art that would be expected of her. Harriet at last agreed reluctantly to learn. She proved an apt pupil. Effy said she would retire from the game and let Harriet take her place and gave her a shilling as a stake. They played faro and silver loo and Harriet won every time. "Beginner's luck," said Amy sourly, for she hated to lose. "You have won sixteen shillings."

"I cannot keep it," said Harriet. "I was not playing with my money."

Mr. Haddon smiled. "Deduct the shilling Miss Effy gave you and give it back to her and keep the rest. You will need some card money for social evenings, you know."

Harriet retired to her room, clutching fifteen whole shillings and feeling decidedly sinful. She spread out the shillings on her toilet-table and looked at them.

It would be wonderful, she thought suddenly, to do something really frivolous and silly with some of the money. She had never spent a penny on anything that was not really necessary. What should she do? Go to Gunter's and have an ice? Pay a shilling to the warden in the Park to feed the deer? At last she decided to leave the house early and hire a hack and go to Exeter Change in the Strand and buy that shilling fan. She would leave the house at ten. No one would be stirring, not even the servants, who kept late hours like their employers, and she did not have any lessons scheduled for the following morning.

At ten the next morning, feeling very brave and adventurous, Harriet walked to Oxford Street and stopped a hackney carriage and asked to be taken to the Strand. She had been told that ladies did not travel in hacks and now she knew why. It was dark and smelly and the floor of the carriage was covered with damp and dusty straw.

She paid off the carriage outside Exeter Change and plunged into the colourful bustle and noise. There were stalls with toys, and stalls with scarves and cheap jewellery, and stalls with all sorts of novelties. She threaded her way through the crowd to the stall that sold fans. The one with the Italian picture was still there.

She had just picked it up and was holding out a shilling to the vendor when a drawling voice at her ear said, "Allow me, Miss Brown. I came here at this ungodly hour with the express purpose of buying that fan for you."

Harriet swung round, startled, and looked up into the green eyes of Lord Charles Marsham, too amazed to protest. He paid for the fan and took it from her hand and asked the vendor to wrap it up. "For you cannot want to use it now unless you need to fan the fog away."

Harriet looked over his shoulder and saw that a thin grey fog was settling down over the Strand.

"I thought you had no money at all," he teased as he led her from the shop.

"I won a certain amount at cards yesterday evening," said Harriet. "I felt it was wicked to be gambling, but the Misses Tribble and Mr. Haddon and Mr. Randolph assured me it was quite the thing provided one did not become addicted to it. I wanted to buy something . . . well, useless . . . for once in my life."

"Did you never buy anything frippery before, Miss Brown?"

"No, never."

"Which grim part of the kingdom do you hail from?"

"Scarborough."

"But Scarborough is full of pleasures."

"My late father, my lord, was a Methodist preacher and a good man. I helped him with the work of the parish. We had very little money, and such as we had went on clothes and food and improving books."

"Allow me to drive you somewhere. Is your day of frivolous spending over?"

"Oh, yes, thank you. I won sixteen whole shillings, but I gave one shilling back to Miss Effy, for she had lent that to me as a stake. I was torn between an ice at Gunter's and that fan. I am glad I chose the fan, although you bought it for me. Are you sure I should accept?"

"Of course. Should I send you diamonds, then you may refuse." He looked at her with a sudden stab of compassion. She certainly did not seem to have had much fun in her life. All elated over a mere win of sixteen shillings, and yet he himself had often seen men winning or losing two or three thousand pounds a night at White's without a flicker of emotion. He had seen a young lord lose his house and estates in one sitting. The young aristocrat had cheerfully passed over his marker (his lawyer the next day had put his inheritance up for sale and had been given instructions to pass on the proceeds to the winner), then he had joined his friends again at White's, although he did not play. He had drunk steadily but calmly. And then he had walked outside, taken a pistol out of his pocket, and had blown his brains out on the steps. The Miss Harriet Browns of this world had more sense, boring people though they might be, he thought. But he reminded himself that Miss Brown needed to be taught a lesson, and that lesson was to make her fall in love with one Lord Charles Marsham.

"I shall take you for an ice at Gunter's," he said.

"I have not yet had breakfast," exclaimed Harriet. "And besides, Gunter's will not be open yet."

"You shall have a delicious ice for breakfast, and Gunter himself may take down the shutters for us if he is still closed."

The fog was closing in, throwing a sooty veil over the town. Link boys flickered through the fog like fireflies. London had become a secretive place, a changed place where it was surely quite in order for Miss Brown to eat an ice for breakfast.

And so, still with that excited feeling of adventure, Harriet climbed into Lord Charles's carriage. This time he had his tiger perched on the back, not a boy, but a wizened little man who looked like the ex-jockey he in fact was. The cat was lying stretched out on the driving-seat, protesting lazily at being moved.

"Tom is getting rather fat," said Harriet, lifting the large cat onto her lap.

"He is a gourmand and likes his delicacies," said Lord Charles. "I went to a friend's house last night and Tom ate his share of buttered toast and drank a dish of China tea, and on his return home, he insisted on thin slices of Westphalia ham."

"That is decadence indeed. A few fish-heads would be better for him."

"I have no doubt," said Lord Charles absently, "but he does yowl so much at the sight of cat's meat of any kind.

He is a parvenu and shuns simple food, as all parvenues do. You have a blob of soot on the end of your nose."

Harriet drew out a handkerchief and then a small bottle of rose-water from her reticule. She moistened the handkerchief and scrubbed her face clean. Lord Charles eyed her bulging reticule with amusement.

"What on earth do you carry in there, Miss Brown?"

"Everything I think I might need."

"Such as?"

"How curious you are! My Bible, my notebook and pencil, handkerchief, rose-water, smelling-salts, rhubarb-pills, needle, thread and scissors, bandages . . ."

"Bandages! We are not in the middle of a war."

"Oh, bandages might come in useful one day. Salve for cuts and burns, a comb . . . let me see . . . a hairbrush, pins, hairpins, pomatum, tinder-box . . ."

"Stop! I have heard enough. And here we are just approaching Berkeley Square before it vanishes into the fog. Gunter himself is there. We are in luck."

Soon Harriet was relishing her first ice which was such a delicious experience, she felt there must be something sinful in the eating of ices.

"Is it not very scandalous of me to be here alone with you?" she asked.

"Not in the slightest."

"You are sure?"

"If I planned to ruin your reputation, Miss Brown, I should go about it in a more imaginative way."

"You sound very rakish," said Harriet sternly. "In fact, I fear you *are* very rakish. Perhaps you are not a suitable gentleman to put ideas of marriage into anyone's head."

"Ideas of marriage are already in my head," he said, smiling into her eyes.

Harriet met his gaze, clear-eyed. "I think we should put

55

our cards on the table, my lord, for I do not like deception. I was prepared to go along with your little game to see if you could be of help to the Tribbles, but I cannot let you continue to behave like this."

"Miss Brown! What can you mean?"

"You find me prudish and judgmental and so you decided it might enliven the tedium of your life if you could make me fall in love with you. In that way, you would enjoy a little gentle sport at my expense and teach me the lesson you think I deserve at the same time."

He looked at her in surprise and then his heavy lids drooped to conceal his expression.

"You underrate your charms, Miss Brown."

"Not I. I do not have any fashionable charms." Harriet let out an infectious gurgle of laughter. "Poor Tribbles. My dancing is appalling. But I will strike a bargain with you. You help me with the Tribbles and I will help you find a pretty little wife."

He felt he ought to be angry, but instead he felt a sort of bubbling amusement growing inside him, mixed with admiration for her shrewdness. He held out his hand. "I agree. Let us shake on it. I can hardly wait to see the sort of female you think suitable for me."

Harriet solemnly took his proffered hand and shook it.

His hand was dry and warm and firm. She looked at his thin, handsome face and felt a little pang of disappointment. What a pity he was not a more worthy character.

Harriet did not like to lie. But she could hardly tell the Tribble sisters that she had allowed Lord Charles to entertain her at Gunter's with a view to seeing the sisters safely married, and so she said mildly that she had spent some of her winnings on taking a hack to the Strand to look at the shops.

She then applied herself to her various lessons with indefatigable zeal until poor Harris, the butler, claimed he was being danced off his feet, but at least Harriet had become used to dancing easily with a man. She then surprised the Tribbles by suggesting they should take her out on calls where she might meet a few other young ladies. "So important to have friends, I think," said Harriet, failing to explain she was wife-hunting for Lord Charles. She could only hope he was performing his part of the bargain and seeking out Mr. Haddon and Mr. Randolph.

Lord Charles ran both the nabobs to earth in Child's coffee-house in St. James's.

He asked permission to join them and then expressed his admiration for the Tribble sisters. "Very game, don't you think," said Lord Charles, "to up and find a means of earning a living? How are they getting on with Miss Brown, and what is her problem apart of being short of the ready?"

Mr. Haddon smiled. "Miss Brown, alas, is such a sterling character that she lacks the necessary frivolity and shallowness considered essential in any young female looking for a husband."

"Perhaps not all men would wish a silly widgeon," said Lord Charles. "You gentlemen, for example, would expect more in the character of any female you chose to wed."

"Unfortunately, we are both hardened bachelors," said Mr. Randolph with a complacent smile.

"Odso!" drawled Lord Charles. "But perhaps that is fortunate."

"How so?" asked Mr. Haddon.

"There are various widowers in London society who have confided to me their admiration of Miss Amy and Miss Effy. Of course, Miss Effy is vastly pretty for her age, but Miss Amy has all the humour and strength of character many a man would admire. Strange as it may seem, it would not surprise me if the ladies had a great success before another year is out and that success will be their own marriages."

Mr. Randolph laughed. "Why, my lord, the Tribbles are as dedicated to spinsterhood as we are to bachelordom."

Lord Charles studied his well-manicured nails. "Now, gentlemen," he chided, "what female of any age is ever dedicated to spinsterhood? Which reminds me. I must call on another of their beaux, although I don't know which one of 'em he fancies, Miss Amy or Miss Effy."

"And who is this gentleman?" asked Mr. Haddon crossly.

"None other than my uncle, Mr. Lawrence," said Lord Charles smoothly. "You will no doubt be meeting him."

Lord Charles took his leave and went straight to his uncle's lodgings. Mr. Lawrence, his mother's brother, had but lately come to Town. He was a well-preserved gentleman of fifty-eight years old, a widower, and addicted to gambling.

He was sitting in his dressing-gown, reading the morning papers and drinking coffee when Lord Charles arrived. Although it was three in the afternoon, he had just risen from bed. He was a pleasant-looking man with the smooth, well-kept appearance of the hedonist who lets nothing trouble him. He had a thick head of white hair, pale-blue eyes, and a small, thin mouth.

"Sit down, Charles," he said, waving an elegant hand at a vacant chair on the other side of the newspaper-strewn table. "Have some chocolate and tell me how you go on."

"Tolerably well," said Lord Charles. "How are your gambling debts?"

"Monstrous," said Mr. Lawrence cheerfully. "Alas, I

shall have to return to the country and rusticate. The duns are bothering my peace of mind."

"I could arrange for you to stay in Town a little longer," said Lord Charles.

"That would be vastly pleasant. How do you mean to do it? By paying my gambling debts?"

"Exactly."

"Dear boy. I am moved." Mr. Lawrence leaned back in his chair and surveyed his nephew with a mixture of cynicism and affection. "And what am I to do in return?"

Lord Charles smiled slowly. "Listen, Uncle dear," he said, "and I shall tell you . . ."

Chapter 4

Yet he was jealous, though he did not show it,
For jealousy dislikes the world to know it.

—*Lord Byron*

I T LOOKED AS IF Harriet Brown
might refuse point-blank to attend her
first London ball. For it was to be a masked ball held at
the Marchioness of Raby's. The late Mr. Brown had
damned all forms of dressing up as licentious and sinful.

It was Yvette, the French dressmaker, who saved the
situation. She arrived at Holles Street with her baby,
George. Harriet thought George a very fine boy indeed.
The sisters retired and left her alone with Yvette. Yvette
had been instrumental in persuading the stern Miss
Brown that it was not sinful to wear fashionable clothes.
Perhaps she could be equally persuasive about fancy
dress.

"Your baby is a handsome, strong boy, Yvette," said Harriet. "Your husband must be very proud of him."

"I have no husband and never did have one," replied Yvette calmly, opening a book of sketches.

"What happened?" asked Harriet bluntly.

Yvette sighed and rested the book on her lap. "There was a French tutor the ladies had hired to school one of their charges. I was very much in love with him and . . . indiscreet. When he ran away and abandoned me, I tried to kill myself, but Miss Amy—ah, the so formidable Miss Amy—she would not let me. She said I must have my baby and she and Miss Effy would help to bring it up. Now, thanks to the generosity of Mr. Kendall, the previous young lady's father, I have my own business, my own salon, and a sound future for George which *I* will make for him."

Now Harriet knew that her father would, on hearing this news, have forbidden her to have anything to do with such a woman. But Amy Tribble had acted with Christian charity. It would have been a supreme act of cruelty to turn Yvette out in the street. Harriet began to feel uneasily that the Tribbles had more genuine charity and kindness in their souls than her late father.

And the Tribbles saw nothing wrong in dressing up for a masked ball. As Miss Amy had pointed out, having fun was as much part of life as sorrow.

"What is the name of this man who betrayed you?" asked Harriet.

"A Monsieur Duclos."

"Is he still in this country?"

"No, miss, I believe he is in Paris working as valet to the Comte De Ville."

"And does he know of his son?"

"No, Miss Brown, and you ask too many questions. Do but look at these pretty sketches and choose one."

"Yvette, I cannot be quite convinced that a masked ball is a respectable event, even though sanctioned by the Misses Tribble."

"La! The whole of the Season is a frivolous game. Why balk at one event? It will be exactly like an ordinary ball and very sedate. The Marchioness of Raby is all that is convenable."

"Are the Misses Tribble going in fancy dress?"

"Yes. Miss Amy wanted to go as a corsair, but I told her that the gentlemen prefer ladies to be dressed as ladies and so she is going as Queen Elizabeth, and Miss Effy is going as a gypsy. I do not suggest you should go in Turkish costume. Everyone in London seems determined to dress as a Turk. I suggest a shepherdess costume."

"No, I cannot countenance the romanticization of shepherdesses."

"Perhaps as a Greek goddess?" Yvette held out a sketch.

"Oh, no!" exclaimed Harriet, recoiling from the drawing of a vision in transparent muslin. "Anything else?"

"Here is a pretty one—queen of the fairies."

"I am not ethereal enough. Wait a moment. I saw something which might serve very well."

Harriet searched among her small stock of books and then opened one at a steel engraving that depicted a young lady in the severe Puritan dress of the reign of Cromwell. "This would do very well," she said.

Yvette spread her hands in a Gallic gesture of resignation. She was very busy and had many fashionable clients, and although her first loyalty lay with the Tribbles, she did not, on the other hand, wish to waste hours in

inappropriately
silly
unnecessary
attention

trying to persuade Miss Brown to wear something more frivolous. She promised to return the following day with some sketches and then went downstairs to prepare Miss Amy and Miss Effy for the forthcoming shock of sponsoring a Puritan maid to her first ball.

"It's the outside of enough!" exclaimed Effy. "Yvette, did you not talk to her of men? Of romance?"

"I never waste words," said Yvette. "I shall make her a most becoming gown. Now I come to think of it, it will serve very well. She will stand out among all the Turks and gypsies and shepherdesses."

"The trouble is, she'll probably act the part to perfection," said Amy gloomily. "What is it, Harris?"

"A Mr. Lawrence has called," said the butler.

Effy looked at Amy and Amy looked at Effy. "Isn't he that gambler?" said Amy at last. "I seem to have heard some talk about him. What does he want, Harris?"

"He appears to be making a call," said the butler.

"Very well," said Amy. "Show him up."

Yvette picked up her baby and took her leave. Before Mr. Lawrence made his entrance, Effy said, "I think Lord Charles has lost all interest in Harriet—not that I think there was much there in the first place. He has not been to call. Still . . ."

She broke off as Mr. Lawrence made his entrance. He carried two huge bouquets of flowers, one of which he presented to Effy and the other to Amy.

"You must forgive my presumption, ladies," said Mr. Lawrence, making a courtly bow. "But I have long admired you from afar. My nephew, Lord Charles Marsham, suggested I call."

Effy fluttered her lamp-blackened eyelashes and begged him to be seated.

"You are too kind, sir," she said.

"I was not prompted by kindness," said Mr. Lawrence. "The day is fine and I have my carriage outside. May I persuade you both to come driving with me?"

"We have a certain Miss Brown to look after," said Amy doubtfully.

"Ah, who has not heard of your school for manners?" Mr. Lawrence kissed the air somewhere above his fingertips. "But you cannot always be working, and the day is fine."

Effy stole a look at the square of grey sky showing through the windows. "I suppose, Amy, it would do no harm," she ventured.

Harris entered again and announced the arrival of Mr. Haddon and Mr. Randolph, who came in hard on his heels and stopped short in surprise at the sight of Mr. Lawrence.

Effy made the introductions. Mr. Lawrence surveyed both gentlemen with severe dislike. Then he turned to Amy. "May I suggest you ladies fetch your bonnets?" he said. "I will make your excuses to these gentlemen."

"What has gone wrong?" demanded Mr. Haddon sharply.

"Nothing," said Mr. Lawrence airily. "I am taking these angels driving in the Park."

Both Mr. Haddon and Mr. Randolph sat down suddenly, side by side, on the sofa. Amy flashed a look at Effy and in that look was all the girlish mischief of years gone by. "Come along, Effy," she said, and urged her startled sister from the room.

Harriet was very cross to learn that both ladies were going out driving with a gentleman of whom she had never heard. Amy and Effy in their excitement forgot to tell her that Mr. Lawrence was Lord Charles's uncle, and so she thought, as she had thought in the recent days

when he had failed to put in an appearance, that Lord
Charles had forgotten about her plans of marriage for the
Tribbles.

Mr. Haddon and Mr. Randolph took their leave with-
out waiting to see the sisters depart on their drive. "Lord
Charles must have been telling the truth," said Mr. Had-
don wonderingly as both men strolled in the direction of
Oxford Street. "Which one do you think he fancies, Miss
Amy or Miss Effy?"

"Bound to be Miss Effy," said Mr. Randolph.

Mr. Haddon walked on for some moments in silence. "I
would not be too sure of that," he said at last. "Miss Amy
has very fetching ways."

Amy and Effy had told Harriet to continue with her
French lessons in their absence, but no sooner had they
gone than a message arrived from the French tutor to say
he was indisposed and so Harriet was free. And then Lord
Charles Marsham made his entrance, the cat at his heels,
a cat that now sported a smart red collar studded with
rubies.

"I do not like Tom in that collar," said Harriet severely.
"It is a stray cat, an undistinguished cat. To dress it up
thus is making a mockery of the animal."

"I am bringing it into fashion, Miss Brown," said Lord
Charles plaintively.

Harriet turned to the butler, who was standing by the
open door of the drawing-room. "Is it quite correct for me
to receive Lord Charles?" she asked the butler.

"Yes, miss. Mrs. Lamont, the housekeeper, is at hand
and I will leave the door of the drawing-room open."

"And now the conventions have been satisfied," remarked Lord Charles when the butler had withdrawn,
"tell me how you go on and why have you not been out
and about in society?"

"I have," said Harriet, "but not to any major event.

66

Alas, I have not met any young female who would suit your taste. But I am to go to the Marchioness of Raby's masked ball."

"I, too, will attend. What are you going as?"

"A Cromwellian lady."

"How eminently suitable."

"I am sure that is not meant as a compliment," said Harriet. "Now, to business. Have you done anything at all about the Misses Tribble?"

"Fie, for shame, Miss Brown, when I just saw both of them driving out with my uncle."

"Your uncle! Mr. Lawrence is your uncle? But he does not have a title."

"My mother's side of the family are very plain."

Harriet smiled on him with such warmth that he blinked. She was always pleased to find her faith in the human race justified. "I knew there was some good in you. If only you were travelling to Paris."

He smiled lazily and patted the cat. "Why Paris, Miss Brown?"

"You could be of such use to me. Have you heard of Yvette, the dressmaker?"

"Of course."

"There is no 'of course' about it," said Harriet tartly. "Gentlemen do not usually know the names of dressmakers."

"You will find in society," said Lord Charles meekly, "that any man worth his salt knows the best dressmakers and the best milliners and the best place to buy feathers . . ."

"Why?"

"In order to be able to converse with the fair sex. I have spent many a happy evening discoursing on the merits of glove-makers."

Harriet looked at him doubtfully. It was hard to understand a man of mature years and good physique who had fought in the wars and yet whose mind appeared to be wholly given over to dissipation and triviality. Still, he had done his best for the Tribbles.

"Yvette," she began, colouring slightly, "has an illegitimate baby. The father is a Monsieur Duclos, now working in Paris as a valet to the Comte de Ville. He is not aware he has a son."

"Allow me to interrupt, Capability Brown. You wish me to ride to Paris and drag the guilty father back to London at the wheels of my chariot?"

"Something like that," said Harriet with a grin.

"There is, however, the post. Had you not thought of writing a letter to this seducer?"

"My French is poor, very poor, and I could hardly ask my tutor to write such a delicate matter for me."

She looked at him pleadingly, her eyes very wide and blue.

Again he felt that bubbling feeling of amusement. "Find me pen and paper, Miss Brown," he said, "and I will write a letter."

Soon he was sitting at an escritoire in the corner of the room while Harriet stood behind him, watching eagerly as he wrote busily. He was conscious of her standing close behind him, he could feel the heat emanating from her body. "Is that the way one spells 'deception'?" he asked. Harriet leaned forward. He had the letter half shielded by his arm. She bent lower until her face was on a level with his own. He could feel a tendril of her hair brushing his cheek.

"Yes, I think so," said Harriet. "It is spelt like the English way, although I suppose you know it means 'disappointment.' From the little French I have learned, I know that much."

He turned his face quickly and kissed her lightly on the cheek. She started back as though he had bitten her and scrubbed at her cheek.

"You should not have done that," said Harriet furiously. "Please leave and never come here again."

He swung round and smiled at her maliciously. "A fine reformer you are, Miss Harriet Brown. You would cast me out and leave me to my old ways. I apologize, but old habits die hard. Now, are you not even curious to know how I coerced my uncle into paying court to the Tribble sisters?"

"Yes, I am curious," said Harriet. "But you must behave yourself in future, my lord. Is that clear?"

"Very clear, ma'am. I am all repentance. I kiss the hem of your gown." He half-rose to his feet.

"No!" said Harriet sternly. "Sit down there and finish that letter and then tell me about your uncle."

"Yes, ma'am." He finished writing, sanded the letter, promised to post it after he had found out the address of the Comte De Ville, and then told her about the bargain he had struck with his uncle.

"Oh, dear," said Harriet. "That sounds a little bit like blackmail."

"No, it is a comfortable arrangement to everyone's satisfaction. The Tribbles will be rejuvenated by his attentions, I assure you."

"We'll see," said Harriet doubtfully. "But I have not asked you how you go on."

"Tolerably, Miss Brown. I spend my nights gambling and drinking deep and my days are passed in recovering from the nights."

She looked saddened and disappointed, so he said quickly, "But of course, this sterling female you are going to find for me will change all that."

"I am beginning to wonder if you should marry at all," replied Harriet.

"But I must! It will be the making of me. And why should I do all the work—writing letters to seducers and persuading my elderly uncle to go courting? It is high time you did something for me."

"I shall try to find you someone," said Harriet. "We are to attend a musicale this evening. Surely there will be someone there. And now I think you should take your leave."

He kissed her hand and left with the cat at his heels.

As he strolled down the steps to his carriage, he noticed a sandy-haired man and a drab-looking female walking up and down. He was sure they had been there the last time he had called.

They noticed his sharp scrutiny and walked quickly away. He stood for a moment looking after them.

From a closed carriage at the corner of the street, Jack Perkins watched his former friend. He would find out who lived at that address.

Miss Spiggs and "Dr." Frank did not speak until they were in Oxford Street.

"He looked at us so strangely," said Miss Spiggs nervously. "Do you think he is suspicious?"

"Shouldn't think so," said Frank. "We'll wait a bit and go back. We now know her name's Harriet Brown and we'll need to hope she comes out alone one day or just with her maid." He patted his pocket, feeling the reassuring bulk of his pistol. "Then, when she does, we simply walk up to her, put the gun in her ribs, and march her off to a hack and take her to our lodgings."

Miss Spiggs shivered with excitement. "And do you think the Tribbles will pay up?" she asked.

"Course," said Frank. "Bound to."

Harriet, hearing the laughing and chattering on the stairs, at first thought some young female friends of the Tribbles had come to call. But it was Effy and Amy themselves, giggling and laughing. "And did you notice the way Mr. Lawrence squeezed my hand?" said Effy. "La, I did not know where to look, sis."

"Which is just as well," said Amy with a grin. "For he immediately pressed my hand when you were looking the other way."

For a moment, Effy looked furious, but then she began to giggle again. "What a rake," she exclaimed. "And he insists on coming with us to the musicale tonight. I told him it was German *lieder*, and he said he doted on the Germans and I am sure he thinks '*lieder*' is the name of a dish."

"I hope Mr. Haddon will not be angry with us," said Amy.

Effy bristled. "He has no right to be angry. Besides, he and Mr. Randolph said they were going to be otherwise engaged."

Both Mr. Haddon and Mr. Randolph had forgotten about the musicale. They arrived at Holles Street that evening, only to learn that the ladies had left for Lady Huxtable's mansion in Berkeley Square.

"Forgot all about it," said Mr. Haddon. He felt very disappointed. He had been looking forward to his usual evening of cards and gossip and flattery. Both gentlemen were turning away when Harris, the butler, added with a certain tinge of satisfaction in his voice, "The ladies were escorted by Mr. Lawrence."

"What is that fool of a mountebank doing dancing attendance on our ladies?" raged Mr. Haddon as they walked off down the street.

"He has gambling debts, I believe," said Mr. Randolph gloomily. He squinted down at his new frilled cambric shirt. It was very fine and he had been looking forward to Miss Effy's flattering comments on his taste.

"Lawrence can't be hoping to make money out of the ladies," said Mr. Haddon, so overset that he tossed a guinea to a crossing-sweeper in mistake for a penny. The boy grabbed the coin, dropped his brush, and ran off whooping with delight into the night.

"Perhaps he really is thinking of marriage." Mr. Randolph was feeling as if an earthquake had rocked his safe world. He had imagined his pleasant life would go on the way it always had, with walks with his friend in the parks and visits to the Tribble sisters.

He waited for Mr. Haddon to pooh-pooh such a suggestion but his friend walked on, his head bent. At last Mr. Haddon said, "We still have our cards for Lady Huxtable's affair, have we not?"

"Yes, I still have mine."

There was another long silence and then Mr. Haddon said, "I feel it is our duty to go and see if the Misses Tribble need our protection."

"Yes, yes, let us go by all means," gasped Mr. Randolph, now quite breathless with trying to keep up with the long angry strides of his tall friend.

It was the very first time Miss Harriet Brown had seen the cream of London society gathered together. Here, she thought bitterly, was no room for reform. With their carefully studied arts and graces and their hard, assessing, arrogant eyes, here was a world of people who would consider the merest suggestion that they were other than perfect the height of impertinence. For the first time, Harriet began to wonder why on earth Lord Charles put up with her. But the thought of Lord Charles reminded her of her mission, and when she left her cloak in an anteroom provided for the occasion and sat down at a toilet-table to tidy her hair, she studied the other young ladies reflected in the glass. One in particular caught her eye. She was tall and modishly gowned. Her brown hair was exquisitely dressed and her beautiful face slightly marred by the hard expression in her eyes. Harriet sensed she was probably shallow and acquisitive but of very good lineage. Harriet thought she would make a good match for Lord Charles; she looked the kind of young lady who would find a rake amusing.

Harriet rose to her feet and arranged her shawl about her shoulders, headed for the door, affected to stumble against the beautiful girl, and apologized profusely.

The young lady's eyes took in the elegance of Harriet's blue-and-grey gown of half mourning. "You are forgiven," she said with a slight smile. "Have we met? I am Lisa Seymour."

"No, I do not think so," replied Harriet. "I am Harriet Brown, one of the Tribble sisters' problems."

Lisa smiled even more warmly. The Tribbles were good ton and the marital success of their charges was well-known.

"You do not look like a problem to me, Miss Brown. What is supposed to be wrong with you?"

"No money and prim manners," rejoined Harriet.

Lisa gave her a startled look and then began to laugh.

"You are an Original, Miss Brown. Shall we endure the tedium of this concert together? And you must introduce me to the legendary Tribbles."

They walked into the music room together.

People were standing around in groups chatting before the start of the concert. "Now where are these old quizzes of yours?" demanded Lisa.

"The Misses Tribble are fine ladies," said Harriet severely. "You must not criticize them or I shall become angry."

"You have very high and mighty airs for a penniless 'problem,' " pointed out Lisa acidly.

"No, I am a loyal friend and could be one to you."

Lisa was about to cold-shoulder this lady whom she was beginning to damn in her mind as an awkward oddity when Lord Charles strolled into the room and came up to join Harriet.

"I am so glad you are come, Lord Charles," said Harriet. "May I present Miss Lisa Seymour."

Lord Charles bowed. "I have already had the pleasure of meeting Miss Seymour."

"Oh." Harriet's face fell. Lisa's eyes darted from one to the other curiously. Lord Charles could not possibly be interested in this Harriet female. She was quite old, surely about twenty-five! But then, despite the nasty rumours that the Tribbles' last charge had eloped with the Duke of Berham to get away from them, she *had* married a duke, and the ones before her had all married well. Lisa had been confined in the country with measles during what was to have been her first Season. That was why she was being brought out at the Little Season. She had had time to study the field and had already decided that Lord Charles Marsham was the most eligible man in Town. He appeared on friendly terms with Miss Brown. It would therefore do no harm to cultivate Miss Brown's friendship.

"Of course," Lord Charles was murmuring, "I rely on your sound advice, Miss Brown."

"You sound as if you share a secret," said Lisa.

"There are no secrets between Miss Brown and myself," said Lord Charles. "Miss Brown is a model of all the virtues." He made those virtues sound like a dead bore and Lisa smiled.

"Perhaps you will allow me to call on you, Miss Brown," Lisa said. "I have no friends in London as yet."

"Gladly." Harriet decided the best thing was to leave the pair alone together. "I must see my chaperones," she said, dropping a curtsy.

She moved off and Lord Charles's eyes followed her across the room. "I wonder who her dressmaker is," said Lisa.

"I can reveal it is none other than Yvette," replied Lord Charles.

"Indeed! I must tell Mama to patronize her. Miss Brown's style puts us all in the shade."

"Nothing," said Lord Charles fervently, "could put such beauty as yours in the shade, Miss Seymour."

Lisa gave a delicious laugh and raised her fan to cover her imaginary blushes. "You are determined to turn my head, Lord Charles."

"Not I! I only speak the truth."

Harriet stole a covert look at the pair from across the room. They appeared to be getting along famously. She felt depressed because all of a sudden twenty-five seemed very old indeed.

Mr. Lawrence was laughing and flirting with both sisters in turn. Amy's great laugh rang across the room and Effy fluttered and simpered and twitched at her gauze draperies. Mr. Haddon and Mr. Randolph made their entrance. Mr. Lawrence saw them arrive out of the corner of his eye and flirted harder than ever.

Amy and Effy both felt glad that for the first time Mr. Haddon and Mr. Randolph could see that someone found them attractive. But it was Amy who remembered their duties first and made her excuses and sought out the Marchioness of Raby.

"I have a new charge, Lucy," she said to the marchioness. "Miss Brown. Over there."

The little marchioness raised her quizzing-glass and studied Harriet. "Fine female," she remarked. "Lots of character in that face. Pity. Looks intelligent. Damning. Mouth too big."

"She has little money and high principles," said Amy.

"Ah, well, you are in luck. I have just the fellow for her. The vicar of our local parish is here. I invited him to stay. Mr. Feathers. Widower. Thirties. Should get married. Come with me."

Amy followed the marchioness to a corner of the music room where a tall, earnest-looking man was talking to an elderly lady.

"Mr. Feathers," said the marchioness, interrupting his conversation without apology. "Step aside."

Mr. Feathers did as he was bid.

"Now, Mr. Feathers," said the marchioness sternly, "you have been a widower for long enough and it don't do to have an unattached man as vicar. Sets all the silly hens of the parish in a flutter. Miss Tribble here will introduce you to a suitable young lady. I'm not ordering you to marry her, mind, but make a push."

"Certainly, my lady," said Mr. Feathers with a sycophantic smile. "You have only to command."

"Disgusting lack of backbone, but what would you?" remarked the marchioness in a loud aside.

Amy eyed Mr. Feathers speculatively. He had a good head of brown hair and a long, not unpleasing face. He was dressed in plain severe clothes of good cut. Her glance flicked down to his legs. Disappointing. But no one expected the clergy to have good legs. "Come with me, Mr. Feathers," said Amy.

He meekly followed her across the room, where she introduced him to Harriet and then left them together.

"Is this the first time you have been in Town, Miss Brown?" asked Mr. Feathers.

"Yes, sir," replied Harriet.

"It must be very exciting to be in society."

"Yes, everyone looks so grand," said Harriet cautiously.

"Have you come from far?"

"Scarborough, Mr. Feathers."

"Ah, but you must have enjoyed many frivolities there."

"On the contrary, my father was a Methodist preacher and I was involved in helping him with the work of the parish."

"How commendable," bleated Mr. Feathers, although he was as shocked as if Harriet had declared herself to be a Roman Catholic. He cast an anguished look in the direction of his patroness, who returned it with a scowl that seemed to tell him to get on with it.

The start of the concert was announced and Mr. Feathers found chairs for both of them. Harriet noticed that Lord Charles was finding chairs for himself and Lisa Seymour and was paying her every attention. She should have felt glad but did not. She put her lowness of spirits down to the strain of her first important social engagement and tried to console herself by turning her attention to Mr. Haddon and Mr. Randolph, who were looking suitably annoyed at the way Mr. Lawrence was fussing about the Tribbles like the best of devoted courtiers. His gambling debts must be immense, reflected Harriet rather sourly. Mr. Feathers was saying something, and she automatically answered, "Yes," and then wondered what he had said, for he looked surprised. It was very lowering to think that Harriet Brown was considered fit consort only for this boring member of the church. Harriet blushed at her own worldliness and wondered whether London was already corrupting her morals. She had never damned anyone as boring in her life before.

"Who is that man with Harriet?" whispered Effy to Amy.

"Vicar," muttered Amy. "Widower. Will do very nicely."

"Do you think so? You know, when Harris told us that Lord Charles had called again, I began to hope . . . Who is that beautiful young lady who has taken his fancy?"

"A Miss Lisa Seymour," said Amy. "Rich parents. New on the market. Don't like the look of her. Looks like a bitch."

"Amy!"

"Fact. And a licentious bitch at that. Some of these young virgins go on like whores. Still, I suppose it's because they don't know any better. Look! She's hitching at her skirt so that he'll get a glimpse of her ankles. Slut!"

"Well, you did say Lord Charles was not suitable," said Effy maddeningly. "So why are you getting into a passion?"

"I'm not getting into a passion," snorted Amy. "I am angry with Mr. Haddon, who keeps looking daggers at me as if I have done something wrong."

"Do you think he is jealous?" asked Effy hopefully.

"Probably indigestion," muttered Amy.

The concert began. The German singer had a beautiful voice that fell on mainly deaf ears as society whispered and shuffled. Harriet sat entranced by the music. Her eyes filled with tears, and Lord Charles, watching her, felt a pang of compassion for this Methodist's daughter who seemed to him to have had a deuced hard life to date. That long-nosed bore she was saddled with was no doubt deemed suitable for her. She would end up married to someone like that, with all that fire and passion wasted. Now why did he assume there was fire and passion in a lady who had recoiled in horror from a kiss on the cheek? But she amused him, and he could not remember when he had last felt amused. He had paid court to Miss Seymour only in the hope of irritating Harriet. But Harriet had not even seemed to notice. After the concert was over, he became tired of the game of flirting with Miss Seymour, hailed his friend, Guy Sutherland, with relief, and slid off, leaving him to talk to her. Lisa watched him go, watched him approach Harriet, say something to the gentleman with her, and then walk off to the supper room with Harriet on his arm. Her beautiful eyes narrowed. She was not going to see the prize of the Little Season taken away from her by someone as old as Miss Brown.

"You cut out Mr. Feathers rather rudely," Harriet was saying crossly. "How am I ever to find a husband if you are not going to allow me any time with suitable beaux?"

He smiled down at her in such a way that she felt weak and breathless. "Come, Miss Brown," he teased. "You were bored to flinders."

"Yes, I was," said Harriet candidly, "and very wicked of me it was too. What is come over me that I should feel bored by someone as kind and worthy as Mr. Feathers?"

"Perhaps common sense."

"What is that rip doing flirting with Harriet again?" said Amy crossly. She then said over her shoulder, "Mr.

79

Haddon, be so good as to approach them and hear what they are saying."

"I am hungry and intend to have my supper," said Mr. Haddon irritably.

Amy swung around to face him. "Then I shall ask Mr. Lawrence," she said sweetly.

"If you find a mountebank and hardened gambler a suitable aide, then by all means ask him," retorted Mr. Haddon.

"I shall," said Amy. "Oh, Mr. Lawrence."

Mr. Haddon strode off.

But Mr. Lawrence, on being appealed to, smiled and shook his head. "I never interfere in my nephew's life," he said. "How can you trouble your head about such things, Miss Amy, when I am present to hang on your every word?"

But Lord Charles was suffering from a more annoying interruption to his conversation with Harriet than his uncle might have supplied. Jack Perkins had arrived late, and now, without waiting for an invitation, joined the couple at their table.

"Good evening, Jack," said Lord Charles pleasantly, after he had made the introductions, "and having said that, I shall bid you good evening again in the hope you will take yourself off."

"Only wanted to know what we are doing tonight," said Jack breezily. "Might drop by Harriet Wilson's later, hey?"

Harriet Wilson, dubbed the Queen of Tarts, was a high-flyer. Lord Charles's eyes turned ice-cold. "I have no intention of frequenting tarts, Jack, and never have had, that you know."

Jack Perkins gave a hearty laugh. "Come, now, Charles, we all know you for a rake."

"You have two seconds to leave this table," replied Lord Charles, "before I call you out."

"You never spoke to me thus before," cried Jack Perkins. *"She* has come between us." He rose so abruptly that his chair went flying and stormed out of the room.

Harriet sat with her face flaming while all sorts of nasty little thoughts buzzed about her brain. One could not read the classics without being aware that there were men who preferred other men above any woman.

Lord Charles looked at her agonized face. "No," he said gently, "I am not. And shame on you for your shocking thoughts."

"Are my thoughts so easily read by you?" asked Harriet.

"Yes, my sweeting."

"You must not call me that."

"Very well, my prim Miss Brown. Have a glass of iced champagne and throw away that lemonade."

"I have no need of anything stronger than lemonade."

"Indeed you have." He signalled to a waiter and ordered champagne.

"Now, drink," he commanded. Harriet opened her mouth to refuse, but those green eyes of his were glinting with amusement and he was leaning towards her and she had a hot sensation that his body was making love to her although he did not touch her. Nervously she raised her glass and took a gulp. The champagne tasted pleasantly innocuous and very refreshing. She finished her glass and drank another, feeling a warm glow spreading through her body.

"What do you think of Miss Seymour?" she asked.

"Divine. I shall always be grateful to you for reintroducing me to her."

"If I can do anything further to help . . . ?"

He felt she deserved to be punished a little. He was perfectly sure Harriet did not like Miss Seymour one bit. "If you could befriend Miss Seymour and further my suit with her, I should be most grateful."

"Gladly," said Harriet, feeling all at once noble and self-sacrificing.

"And you will do everything to further my cause?"

"Yes," said Harriet bleakly.

"Then have some conversation with her and come driving with me tomorrow. I promise to be sober."

Harriet drank some more champagne. "Why should you wish to drive with me when you are courting her?" she asked.

"So that you may tell me what she thinks of me," he replied gently.

So after supper, when people were strolling about and chatting, Harriet dutifully sought out Lisa, who welcomed her effusively. *excessive in emotional expression*

"Dear Miss Brown," cried Lisa. "I have not told you, but I am a good whip and have my own carriage. You must come driving with me tomorrow."

"I am already engaged to go driving with Lord Charles."

Something far from lovely flashed at the back of Lisa's eyes. "The fact is," went on Harriet, mindful of her duties, "I think it is because he wishes to further his acquaintance with you. I am to sound you out."

Lisa slid an arm about Harriet's waist. "You funny thing," she said. "I declare I quite dote on you already. You must tell him, let me see, that I have many suitors, and that you are not quite sure if my affections are engaged or not."

"If you are interested in him," said Harriet baldly, "would it not be better to allow me to tell him so?"

"No, no, stoopid. It never does to let the gentlemen

know we are keen. They must be played like fish. I believe he is quite rich."

"Yes," said Harriet, fighting down a feeling of distaste. "So I believe."

"Good. My parents would never forgive me if I became enamoured of a *poor* man. Here is *your* beau, Harriet. I may call you Harriet, may I not? I feel we have known each other a lifetime."

Mr. Feathers came up and claimed Harriet's attention. He began to talk about his parish duties and Harriet tried to listen, but all the champagne she had drunk was making her feel sleepy and she found it very hard not to yawn.

The following morning, Harriet awoke early with a feeling of desolation. She could not think what was the matter. She was normally of an optimistic temperament. She rose from bed and washed and dressed and sat down and looked at those shillings which were still lying spread out. She then looked at her appointment book. Effy and Amy had said they preferred to sleep late, and so lessons had been changed to the afternoons. There were the piano teacher at one and the Italian tutor at two, and then Lord Charles at three. When they had found out about the proposed drive, Amy and Effy had lectured Harriet on the folly of encouraging the attentions of a rake who did not have marriage in mind. She was instructed to tell Lord Charles firmly that in future her afternoons would be taken up with either lessons or social calls.

She had a sudden longing to escape from the house and walk by herself for a little. She could take a hack to St. James's Park and look at the guns and walk under the trees.

Feeling more cheerful now that she had decided on a course of action, Harriet put on her cloak and bonnet and made her way downstairs.

Outside in Holles Street, Miss Spiggs shivered in the frosty morning. "I do not know what we are doing here this early, Dr. Frank," she said plaintively. "No one will be stirring."

"I am waiting to see if some servant that don't know me emerges," said Frank. "That way we might fall into conversation and get some news of the comings and goings of Miss Harriet Brown."

Miss Spiggs suddenly clutched his arm tightly. "Look!" she cried. "Is that not she?"

"By all that's holy," breathed Frank. "Come on. This is it."

Turning quite white with excitement, Miss Spiggs followed him across the street.

At first Harriet did not see them. She had recognized a familiar figure turning the corner of the street. Mr. Feathers. She was sure it was he.

But she was reluctant to give up her planned adventure. She would walk quickly in the other direction and find a hack.

She had only taken a few paces when Miss Spiggs and Frank closed in on either side of her. "Miss Brown," hissed Frank. "I have a pistol here. One word from you, one scream for help, and I will shoot you dead."

"Yes, shoot you dead," echoed Miss Spiggs shrilly.

Harriet felt the hard point of the gun at her side.

At that moment a hack came along the street and Frank waved it down with his free hand.

Too startled and frightened to resist, Harriet allowed herself to be pushed inside.

Mr. Feathers tilted back his hat and watched the disappearing hack. It was all most odd. He had strolled along to get a look at the Tribbles' house with a vague idea of assessing the social position of his intended. The Marchioness of Raby was fond of the Tribbles and had promised him a handsome payment if he married Harriet Brown. What had she being doing up so early? And who were these odd people who had marched her off? He had noted the number of the hack, for he always noticed things like that. He decided to call on her later and pay his respects. Still, the marchioness ought to be informed of the odd company she kept. The man with her had been foppishly dressed in a low-class way, not the sort of person the future Mrs. Feathers should be seen with!

Chapter 5

*He flung himself from the room, flung himself
upon his horse and rode madly off in all
directions.*

—Stephen Leacock

AMY ENTERED HER SISTER'S bedchamber later that morning. "We really must discuss this friendship of Harriet's with Lord Charles," she said, plumping herself down so heavily on the bed that the cup of chocolate which Effy was holding in her hand rattled in its saucer.

"Don't be so violent, sister," said Effy crossly.

Amy peered at Effy's face. "What have you been doing to yourself, Effy?" she demanded. "You have an odd circle of white skin around your mouth. It makes you look like a chimpanzee."

Effy put down her cup on a side-table by the bed and lifted a hand mirror and scrutinized her face. She let out a dismayed squawk. "Now what am I going to do? It was a new depilatory. I made it up myself from a mixture of barium sulphide and starch."

"You're supposed to leave these things on for about three minutes."

"Three minutes! Amy, I am sure the instructions said three hours. That book over there."

Amy rose and fetched a notebook bulging with handwritten recipes for beauty treatments. "Here we are," she said, after searching through the pages, "three minutes, plain as plain. You ought to wear spectacles the whole time."

"I will die before I wear spectacles," said Effy. "I shall simply put on some paint . . ."

"As usual," interrupted Amy maliciously.

". . . and no one will know the difference. Yes, something must be done about Harriet. Sensible suitors such as Mr. Feathers will be put off if she is constantly in the company of a rake."

"And yet, it would be a triumph for us," said Amy wistfully, "if we managed to match the penniless daughter of a Methody with a rich aristocrat. We would be really famous."

"But he is not suitable for Harriet. You must see that."

"Well . . ." Amy bit her nails. "What if he genuinely liked her? I mean, what if there is a splendid match under our noses and we are about to spoil it by being overzealous on Harriet's behalf? Now, he is a jaded man of the world, and what is the most interesting thing to a jaded man?"

"Nothing."

"There is something . . . forbidden fruit. We tell him when he calls that we do not approve of him and that Harriet is too good for him and he must never see her again."

"And what if he obeys us?"

"Then Harriet will be free from his company and if he persists in seeing her, then we will know he is genuinely interested in her."

There came a scratching at the door and a footman entered, holding a letter. "This came by hand, ma'am," he said, handing it to Amy.

"So, as I was saying," went on Amy, crackling open the letter and glancing idly down at its contents. Then she went very still and the hand holding the letter began to tremble.

"What is it?" cried Effy in alarm.

Amy threw down the letter and ran from the room to Harriet's bedchamber and flung open the door. No one. She called for the servants and asked them to search the house from top to bottom.

When she returned to Effy, Effy had read the letter and was now lying back against her pillows with Baxter, the lady's maid, holding burnt feathers under her nose. Amy picked it up and read it again. "We have Miss Brown," she read. "It will cost Five Thousand Pounds to have her returned to you, Unharmed. Do not contact the Authorities or we will kill her bit by bit. You Are Being Watched. You will hear from Us again Tomorrow. The Common Man's Avenger."

"Mr. Haddon," said Amy. "Fetch Mr. Haddon."

But the footman who conveyed the message by word of mouth merely said that Miss Amy wanted to see him immediately, and Mr. Haddon, who was in a sulk because of the encouraged attentions of Mr. Lawrence, sent back a message that he was too busy.

Now Amy did feel helpless. She wrote a note, telling him what had happened, and begging for his support and sent it back, but by this time Mr. Haddon had gone out for a walk and was not to be found. Mr. Randolph could not be found either. In despair, Amy sent a letter to Mr. Lawrence, who was taking tea with his nephew, Lord Charles, when the letter arrived.

"Dear me," said Mr. Lawrence, startled out of his usual calm. "Your ladies, the Tribbles, my boy, say here that Miss Brown has been taken by force and her abductors are holding her to ransom."

Lord Charles felt exactly as if someone had just kicked him in the stomach.

He seized the letter and scanned its contents and then jerked his uncle forcibly to his feet. "Come along," he said.

"But I have not had my breakfast," wailed Mr. Lawrence as he was propelled down his staircase. "And it is only two in the afternoon, bedemned."

They found a sad scene in the Tribbles' drawing-room. Amy was sitting by the fire, tears cascading down her face, and on her lap lay a long tress of midnight-black hair.

"They sent this, the murderers," whispered Amy brokenly. "It arrived a few moments ago. What are we to do?"

"How much do they want?" asked Mr. Lawrence, sitting down beside her on the sofa and putting an arm around her shoulders.

"Five thousand pounds," said Effy. "Where are we going to get five thousand pounds?"

"As to that, I will give you the money," said Mr. Lawrence grandly.

Effy threw herself into his arms, nearly sending him flying backwards over the sofa and babbling that he was a hero, a knight in shining armour.

"I do have the money, do I not, nephew?" Mr. Lawrence asked Lord Charles.

"Yes, indeed," said Lord Charles, correctly understanding that it was he who was meant to pay the ransom.

"But why should we give in?" demanded Mr. Lawrence. "Call out the constables. Call out the militia!"

Amy stroked the hair on her lap and miserably shook her head.

"Mr. Feathers," announced Harris.

Mr. Feathers had called earlier than he had intended. He blinked at the distraught faces that met his inquiring gaze and asked timidly, "Is Miss Brown at home?"

"No, she is not," said Mr. Lawrence. "She has been abducted and held to ransom."

"Oh," said Mr. Feathers weakly, "I see I am called at an unfortunate time. When she returns, present my compliments to Miss Brown and—"

"You feeble-minded whoreson. You pig's arse in a dog collar," roared Amy. She held up the hank of hair. "She is being returned to us in *pieces!*"

Mr. Lawrence let out a nervous giggle and then clapped his hand over his mouth in embarrassment.

"As I said," bleated Mr. Feathers, "I must go. You . . . you will probably find it was all a joke and she has simply gone for a drive in a hack with those friends of hers and—"

Lord Charles strode across the room and seized the unfortunate vicar by the lapels of his coat. "You saw her! When did you see her?"

"Unhand me, sir," cried Mr. Feathers, striving for dignity, "and I will tell you."

Lord Charles released him. Mr. Feathers huffily brushed down his coat and said in his finicky voice, "I was taking the air this morning and I saw Miss Brown entering a hack with a woman on one side of her and a man on the other."

"What did they look like?" demanded Lord Charles.

"The woman was shabby-genteel, like a governess or companion. The man was showily and cheaply dressed."

"Height, demme, and colour of hair?" asked Lord

91

Charles, fighting down a longing to shake the information out of the vicar.

"The man was quite tall, with a rabbity sort of mouth and ginger hair."

"Frank the footman," said Amy bitterly. "I'll kill him."

"Who is this footman?" Lord Charles swung round to face Amy.

"He was once in our employ," said Amy. "He left after trying to stop the staff working by filling their heads with a lot of radical nonsense. I saw him earlier this year down in a street near the City. He had been inciting the crowd by preaching the rights of man. He calls himself Dr. Frank now."

"The hack," cried Lord Charles. "Is there any hope you saw the number, Mr. Feathers?"

Mr. Feathers smiled complacently. "I always notice numbers and things like that. I am very observant."

"Well, stop standing there grinning and come out with it," snarled Lord Charles.

Mr. Feathers backed away a step. "It was three-five-three, as I recall," he said.

"I am going in search of that hack," said Lord Charles. "Do not do anything until I return."

"Please be careful," begged Amy. "That Frank is a monster!"

Harriet sat on a hard chair in a bleak room in Blooms-bury and surveyed Miss Spiggs with disfavour. Harriet's hair, minus that one tress, fell about her shoulders. Miss Spiggs was gingerly holding the pistol Frank had left with her.

"Are you man and wife—you and that popinjay?" asked Harriet contemptuously.

"Dr. Frank and I have an understanding," said Miss Spiggs proudly.

"Then you should not be living with him under the same roof, let alone being engaged in criminal activities. What do you plan to do with the money for my ransom, should you ever get it?"

"We shall give it to our fellow sufferers."

"You mean other criminals?"

"No, we are trying to redress the unequal balance among the classes, just like they did in France. Ah, those brave people storming the Bastille and throwing open the prison doors to let their suffering comrades go free. I would love to have been there!"

"You are old enough to have done so," said Harriet with a rare flash of feminine malice. "But what fustian you do talk! They attacked the Bastille, not for the pur- pose of freeing a handful of aristocrats and madmen, but to get at the arsenal that was housed there."

"That is not true!"

"And if you are so concerned with the unequal balance of things, may I suggest you sell that fine diamond pin you are wearing and give some money to the poor?"

Miss Spiggs put one hand protectively up to cover the diamond pin, her prized possession that had been given to her by the Tribbles' last charge, Miss Maria Kendall. Did she somehow guess that her pin was her attraction for Dr. Frank? She did not know Frank was married to the Trib- bles' former maid Bertha, and that Bertha had allowed Frank to go off with Miss Spiggs only because Frank had promised to get that pin; but somewhere deep inside she did not trust Frank, although at that moment she would not have admitted such a dreadful thought to herself.

"Do you know how to use that?" asked Harriet, point- ing to the gun.

Miss Spiggs's eyes flashed. She saw herself on the barricades, leading the revolution. "Of course."

"How did you know of the Misses Tribble?"

Miss Spiggs frowned. She was a plump little woman whose mouth was perpetually curved in a humourless smile.

"I was companion to the last young lady they had in their charge, and it was I who was instrumental in getting the Duke of Berham to marry my lady, Miss Kendall. Both those Tribbles put it about that I had lied and interfered. Mr. and Mrs. Kendall subsequently employed me, but again the Tribbles had me turned off."

"So you do not believe any of that fustian you were talking," said Harriet contemptuously. "You are party to the abduction of me out of no higher motive than plain spite and greed."

Miss Spiggs sniffed haughtily. "It is no use in trying to talk to such a closed mind as yours."

"What are you really going to do with the ransom money?"

Miss Spiggs's pale eyes grew dreamy. "The money will go to the cause, but we shall keep a little for ourselves and buy a cottage in the country and perhaps keep a few pigs and geese."

"So," said Harriet coldly, "you plan to murder me as soon as you have the money."

Miss Spiggs's eyes flashed. "Dr. Frank said he would release you as soon as the ransom is paid, and he is a gentleman."

"Well, you poor fool, and how did you imagine you would be left in peace to enjoy this cottage? All the constables and militia of England will be looking for you."

There was a long silence while the import of what

Harriet had just said sank into Miss Spiggs's silly, besotted brain.

"Then you must promise not to talk," she said weakly.

"Idiot," rejoined Harriet. "Come shoot me now, for I would rather be killed by you than cut into pieces by that red-haired pig."

"Stay where you are!" cried Miss Spiggs as Harriet rose stiffly to her feet, stiff for she felt she had been sitting in that chair for a lifetime. The very act of moving gave her courage. Miss Spiggs leaped to her feet and darted behind her own chair. "Stand back," she shouted.

"If God wishes me to die," said Harriet half to herself, "then I shall die." She closed her eyes for a moment and when she opened them again they were like blue steel.

After what seemed ages, Lord Charles tracked down the driver of the hack, who turned out to be very old and very deaf but whose hearing improved amazingly at the sight of a gold guinea.

"Havers Street," he said. "Don't 'zactly recall the number, but it's slap-bang next to the Gold Lion."

Lord Charles drove off, refusing to think of the peril Harriet was in, determined only to reach Havers Street as quickly as possible.

He reached the Gold Lion pub and tied his horses' reins to a post and went into the pub. The landlord was behind the small cubby-hole of a bar. "Five guineas for you, landlord," said Lord Charles, "if you can tell me the whereabouts of a tall man, foppishly dressed, with ginger hair, who lives hard by."

"Give me the money," said the landlord with a grin, "and I'll tell you."

Lord Charles handed over the money, saying in his pleasant voice, "If you are lying to me, my good man, I will break your head."

"Not I, guv. The man you want is over there, in the corner."

Lord Charles swung round. Frank was indeed there, his eyes unfocused with all he had drunk. He had been drinking and dreaming of how he would take Bertha to France as soon as he got the money. He would kill Harriet, take Miss Spiggs's pin from her, lock her up and leave her to the tender mercies of the magistrates, should they ever find her. He had never killed anyone before, but the drink he had consumed had persuaded him he would be able to do it.

The next thing he knew, he was jerked up to his feet and a pair of blazing green eyes bored into his own.

"Where is Harriet Brown?" said Lord Charles.

Sobered and desperate with fear, Frank tore himself free. He knocked over the table and tried to head for the door. Lord Charles seized him by the coat and swung him around and punched him hard, full on the jaw. Frank staggered and reeled, blood from a cut made by Lord Charles's ring pouring from the side of his mouth. "I'll never tell you," he said. "Come, boys," he yelled to the taproom, "here's some fine lord attacking a decent common man!"

He blinked and shook his head like a baffled bull, for the taproom had emptied and the landlord was crouched down behind the safety of the bar.

Lord Charles swung his fist and punched Frank hard again.

Frank clutched his chest. "Don't," he whined. "My heart. Don't."

Lord Charles got him by the throat and began to shake

him. "Where is she?" he shouted. "Tell me or I will kill you."

Frank gave a strange rattling sound and went limp. Lord Charles let him slide to the floor and strode up to where the landlord was hiding. "Give me a pitcher of water, damn you, till I revive this cur."

The landlord scrambled to his feet and handed over a jug of water and then timidly crept out of his cubicle and from behind the tiny bar and followed Lord Charles across the taproom. Lord Charles dashed the pitcher of water full in Frank's face, but the ex-footman did not move.

"Begging your parding, my lord," said the landlord with an apologetic cough. "But it's my belief you killed 'im."

"Nonsense." Lord Charles knelt on the floor and loosened Frank's collar. He unbuttoned one of Frank's two flowered waistcoats and felt for his heart. Then he slowly rose to his feet. "Pity," said Lord Charles. "It seems you have the right of it. Where did this creature live?"

"Next door," said the landlord, backing away. "Forty-two. Second floor."

"Get away from me," Miss Spiggs was screaming as Harriet advanced menacingly on her. Harriet leaped forward and seized the hand that held the gun. Miss Spiggs, thinking wildly of how angry Frank would be, fought like a tiger, but she was no match for Harriet, who was fighting for her life.

"There!" said Harriet triumphantly. She wrested the gun from Miss Spiggs and backed away. Miss Spiggs stared at her in horror. In a flash, she realized Frank would never forgive her. She would be alone for the rest of her life, no more adventure, no more excitement. With a cry, she darted forward and threw herself on Harriet. There was a deafening report as the pistol went off and Miss Spiggs crumpled to the floor, blood spreading across the front of her gown.

Harriet stood stricken, the smoking pistol in her hand. She heard footsteps pounding up the stairs, heard someone rattling at the door-handle, and then, with an almighty crash, the door burst open and Lord Charles hurtled into the room.

He stopped short and looked gravely down at the dead Miss Spiggs and then solemnly at Harriet, who stood white-faced and glittering-eyed, with her hair cascading about her shoulders.

"I have killed someone," said Harriet. "It was an accident. God forgive me."

"Come with me," he said. "Come away. You are safe and I have found you. Come, my brave girl."

He went forward and caught her as she fell and picked her up in his arms. Frightened faces peered in at the open door.

"This lady has fainted," said Lord Charles. "Tell the constable that Lord Charles Marsham will answer all questions."

Harriet recovered consciousness as he carried her to his carriage. Tears started to her eyes. "Gently, now," he said. "There's my brave girl."

Ignoring the staring crowd that had gathered, he lifted her up into the seat, unhitched his team and drove off just as the angry rattle of the watch sounded at the end of the street.

Fog had closed down, yellow choking fog, blotting out the buildings, turning London into a nightmare City. "Stop the carriage," cried Harriet in a shaky voice. He cast an anxious glance at the white blur of her face and slowed the open carriage to a halt.

Harriet leaped down and then he could hear dismal retching sounds from the back of the carriage. He got down himself, but she pleaded, "Don't come near me. I am so ashamed."

His voice came to her from out of the enveloping fog. "I am here, nonetheless. Do you feel better? I am anxious to get you home."

Harriet came towards him and once more he helped her up.

"I am all right now," she said faintly. "How did you find me?"

"Your Mr. Feathers saw you being taken away and made a mental note of the number of the hack."

"That poor, unfortunate woman," said Harriet, meaning Miss Spiggs. "What happened to that horrible red-haired man?"

"He is dead. An accident. I was trying to find your whereabouts and tracked him down to the Gold Lion. I hit him and threatened him. He had an apoplexy. It is better this way. Both would have hanged and you would have had to endure the rigours of giving evidence at their trial."

Harriet put her hands over her face and shivered. What a bleak world of violence. She slowly lowered her hands and stole a look at her companion. She could barely see him, although he was seated close to her, the fog was so thick. But what she could see revealed the usual lazy, elegant man that was Lord Charles Marsham. She could not imagine him hitting anyone or threatening anyone. And yet he had kicked down the door to rescue her, splintering the lock and leaving it hanging crazily on its hinges. She wanted to go home and then realized she really did not have a home. For the first time she wondered what would happen to her if she did not marry. Lady Owen might keep her as a sort of poor unpaid companion but was more likely to wash her hands of her and damn her as a failure. She was sure the Tribble sisters were fond of her, and yet she was a client to them. They had to earn their living and therefore could hardly be expected to support a dependant.

"What is the time?" asked Harriet.

"Five o'clock."

"It seems a lifetime since I was taken away."

"Apart from cutting off a piece of your hair, did that monster harm you in any other way?"

"No, but he threatened to. He said he would send them a letter this evening, telling them a time and a place to hand over the money tomorrow, and if he returned without the money, then he would send them one of my fingers."

"My poor heart," he said, and at the sound of his voice Harriet's own heart leaped wildly, as she thought first it was an endearment and then settled down as she convinced herself he must have been joking about the state of his own heart.

"I am most grateful to you for trying to help me," she said.

"You had helped yourself by the time I arrived, Capability Brown."

"No, no. If you had not attacked that dreadful man, he might have returned while I was still struggling with that woman."

"Kind of you to say so, but I am not exactly your knight in shining armour. Alas, such capable ladies as yourself do not need us weak men to ride to the rescue."

"I would not like you to think I was missish."

"No, Miss Brown, you are not missish in the slightest."

"Thank you," said Harriet, although she was sure, coming as it did from him, that it was not meant as a compliment.

He drove on, inching his way through the fog, wondering, too, what was to become of Harriet Brown. She would either marry some man like Feathers or return to Scarborough and to good works.

And why am I sneering at the very idea of good works? he then chided himself. Is it because I fear this lady is superior to me in every way?

By the time they arrived at Holles Street, Harriet was beginning to shiver uncontrollably.

The front door flew open before they could reach it, the sisters, demented with worry, having been watching from the window. Not only were Amy and Effy there, but Mr. Haddon, Mr. Randolph, Mr. Lawrence, and Mr. Feathers, who had not been allowed to leave in case Lord Charles returned and wanted to question him further.

Harriet was hugged fiercely by first Amy and then Effy. She could never in her life remember anyone hugging her before.

Mr. Randolph and Mr. Lawrence were crying noisily to show their sensibility, but Mr. Haddon was grim-faced.

He had arrived after Lord Charles had left, to be met with the tears and fears of the Tribbles and to have it explained to him that Mr. Lawrence had volunteered to be the sisters' saviour.

Mr. Haddon was set in his ways. He did not like change. He was overjoyed that Miss Brown was safe, but at the same time he saw a future without any more comfortable evenings with the Tribbles.

Lord Charles suggested Harriet be put to bed immediately and took his leave.

Harriet was borne upstairs. Amy ordered a bath of hot

scented water to be drawn for her and, mindful of Harriet's modesty, left her alone to bathe in peace but with a large handbell beside the bath "in case you come over faint."

When Harriet was at last in bed, Amy and Effy came in carrying a hot drink, followed by Baxter, who put extra blankets on the bed. Then the sisters questioned Harriet, exclaiming in horror to learn that Miss Spiggs had been a party to the plot.

Amy cut short Harriet's tearful regrets over the killing of Miss Spiggs. "Better than watch the wretched woman hang," she said robustly. "We owe a great debt to Lord Charles Marsham, although I gathered you saved yourself, but at least he got rid of Frank. Never could stand that young man. Now you must lie back and sleep. Lord Charles will no doubt be round here with a magistrate, but we will tell whatever authority that arrives that you are not to be disturbed until the morrow. Dear Mr. Lawrence. We were at our wits' end as to how to raise the ransom money and he promptly offered to pay it while that wretched Haddon did not even trouble to call."

"But he is here now," protested Harriet.

"He did not get my note until later, but he should have come the first time he was summoned. Unfeeling brute," sniffed Amy.

Harriet looked at the two sisters, at Amy's honest horselike face, at Effy's faded pretty one, at their concern and love, and her eyes filled with tears again. She was only one of their clients, and yet they had shown her more love than anyone had ever done before. She must do her best for them. They did not know that Lord Charles had inveigled Mr. Lawrence into paying court to them. What if the plan had already backfired and both sisters had fallen in love with the uncle and forgotten their beaux?

"Send Mr. Haddon to me," said Harriet faintly.

"Mr. Haddon! If you are thinking of thanking anyone, then it should be Mr. Lawrence you want to see," pointed out Effy.

"No. I wish to have a private word with Mr. Haddon. Please do not ask questions. It is Mr. Haddon I wish to talk to. Just for a few moments, and then I will go to sleep."

The sisters left after only a few more protests, and eventually Mr. Haddon came into the room. "Shut the door behind you," ordered Harriet feebly, for she was beginning to feel warm and drowsy and longed to sleep.

The nabob did as he was bid and then approached the bed.

"Now turn about smartly and open the door again," ordered Harriet.

Mr. Haddon again did as she ordered and started back as the Tribble sisters, who had been leaning on the other side, nearly fell across the threshold.

"I wanted a *private* word with Mr. Haddon," said Harriet sternly, and so the sisters left, after protesting that Effy had dropped a pin right by the door and all they had been doing was stoop to look for it.

Mr. Haddon approached the bed again. He looked down at Harriet and reflected that it might not be too amazing if Lord Charles was really interested in her. She was not beautiful by accepted standards, but her eyes were fine and her mouth was generous and sensual.

"Bring forward a chair and sit down," said Harriet wearily. "Why did you not call on the sisters when you were first summoned?"

Mr. Haddon frowned. He found the question impertinent, but Harriet looked so weak and ill, he did not like to upset her by refusing to answer her. "I did not know the severity of their problem," he said stiffly. "I was too busy. I then went out for a walk and did not receive Miss Amy's letter until later. I came as soon as I got it. It is ridiculous to believe that Lawrence could ever pay such a sum. He is a gambler and has not a feather to fly with."

"But Lord Charles is very rich, I believe," murmured Harriet. "No doubt Mr. Lawrence knew he would foot the bill."

"Of course!" Mr. Haddon's face cleared. "I must tell Miss Amy."

"It won't do any good," said Harriet. "You will only look churlish. Mr. Lawrence was prepared to find the money, and even if it came from his own nephew it will not diminish his glory one whit. And why should you care?"

Mr. Haddon sat in silence, his face unreadable in the lamplight.

"Please humour me," said Harriet with a wan smile.

"I suppose I *am* being churlish," said Mr. Haddon with a sigh. "I do not like change. I enjoy my life. I enjoy Mr. Randolph's friendship and our visits to the Misses Tribble. I wish things did not have to change. According to Lord Charles, Lawrence is set on marriage, although which one he prefers, I do not know."

"Your life need not change," said Harriet gently. "There is no reason why it cannot go on as it is now, but with one simple alteration."

"That being?"

"If you married Miss Amy and Mr. Randolph married Miss Effy, then you could continue your walks and visits to the club and then come home to the sisters, your wives."

Mr. Haddon began to laugh. "I? Marry Miss Amy? Don't be ridiculous."

"Then, in that case, I shall do everything in my power to discourage your visits and encourage those of Mr. Lawrence," said Harriet crossly.

"But . . ."

"No. No more," said Harriet. "Go away. My head hurts."

Mr. Haddon descended to the drawing-room. There was no one there, but he heard the sound of voices rising from the ground floor and went on down. Amy, Effy, Mr. Lawrence, Mr. Feathers, and Lord Charles were in a saloon to the left of the hall with a magistrate, a beadle, a watchman, and two constables.

Mr. Lawrence seemed to be holding the floor and was being deferred to by the magistrate. Useless old roué, thought Mr. Haddon spitefully as he noticed Amy hanging on Mr. Lawrence's every word. He felt old and cross and wanted to go home, but felt obliged to wait politely until the forces of law and order had been dealt with before suggesting to Mr. Randolph that they take their leave. As they walked out, two gentlemen of the press were being ushered in, one from *The Times* and one from *The Morning Post.* Mr. Haddon half-turned to go back, but reflected that it was wise of the sisters to give the press their version, otherwise a story based on scandal and rumour would appear, and he could not bear to stay and see Mr. Lawrence pontificating and acting as the hero of the day again. → speaking in a pompous way.

Little Mr. Randolph trotted alongside his tall friend, glancing nervously up from time to time at his set face. The fog had thinned slightly and the shadows cast by the parish lamps transformed Mr. Haddon's face into a hard geometric pattern of black and white planes.

"Let us go to Brother's Coffee House for a bottle of something," said Mr. Haddon at last. "Or several bottles."

"You are upset. What did Miss Brown say?" asked Mr. Randolph.

"I would rather tell you when I have had several glassfuls of wine to fortify me" was the reply.

Mr. Randolph became increasingly worried. He knew his friend to be a man of sober habits, enjoying an occasional glassful of wine, but not given to tippling whole bottles.

Once seated in the coffee-house with the bottle between them, Mr. Haddon began. "I declare I do not know whether to laugh at what Miss Brown said to me or be furious at her impertinence. But I must remember she is an ingénue and not accustomed to the ways of the world."

"What did she say?" demanded Mr. Randolph impatiently.

"I was regretting the incursion of Lawrence into our well-ordered lives. It looks as if our friendly evenings at Holles Street are going to come to an end. Of course, I realize Miss Brown was suffering badly from shock, but she pointed out, very coolly, mind, that our lives need not change at all. I should marry Miss Amy, and you, my dear friend, Miss Effy."

Mr. Randolph took out his quizzing-glass, polished it furiously on his sleeve, and raised it to survey the expression on his friend's face better.

"And what did you reply?" he asked.

"I laughed at the very idea. The minx said then that she would do her best to discourage our visits and encourage the visits of Mr. Lawrence."

Mr. Randolph put away his quizzing-glass, took out a lace-edged handkerchief and mopped his brow, fussily tugged down his swansdown waistcoat, took out an enamelled snuff-box and helped himself to a hearty pinch, raised his glass and drained it and filled it up again, drank that, and then said, "You should not have laughed for me."

"What on earth are you talking about?"

"I mean you laughed at the idea on behalf of us both. I shall do my own laughing, if you don't mind," said Mr. Randolph, becoming visibly angrier by the minute.

"My dear friend . . ."

"It is a shock, you see, to think of marriage after having evaded it for so long. But is it such a ridiculous notion? It might be quite jolly. I do not like the idea of poor little Miss Effy working for a living. She has had too many frightening adventures for a lady of her sensibility. Admittedly, the case of Miss Amy is different. *She* is as strong as a man and well able to take care of herself . . ."

"Nonsense. She is capable of getting into more scrapes than a schoolboy."

"So, I repeat, you should not have laughed, or you should have explained your nasty jeering laughter was for Miss Amy, not Miss Effy."

"You are becoming more and more ridiculous," said Mr. Haddon testily.

"I am not. I am not! Miss Brown will tell the ladies how you laughed, and they will continue to fawn on that ridiculous old fop, Lawrence, and it will be all your fault." Mr. Randolph's eyes filled with tears.

"Do you really mean to say you would consider the idea of marriage?" asked Mr. Haddon, amazed.

"Of c-course," hiccuped Mr. Randolph. "I am going to go the proper way about it. I am going to court Miss Effy, and Lawrence can have Miss Amy if he wants!"

He collected his hat, cane, and gloves. "Where are you going?" asked Mr. Haddon.

"I am going to buy a bouquet of flowers, and I am going to send them as soon as possible. The shops are open until ten."

Mr. Haddon watched him go and then refilled his glass. He thought of all the adventures he had had with Amy. He thought of Amy married to Lawrence, not free from worry about money, but doomed to spend an itinerant life travelling with her spendthrift husband from one rich relative's home to another while he borrowed and borrowed to pay his gambling debts. Then Mr. Haddon summoned the waiter and complained that the wine was sour.

Chapter 6

*Set me a seal upon thine heart, as a seal upon
thine arm: for love is strong as death; jealousy
is cruel as the grave.*

—The Song of Solomon

*J*ACK PERKINS SAT IN his lodgings
with the newspapers spread about him.
He had read the account of Harriet's abduction several
times. Alas for Mr. Lawrence. Everybody loves a lord and
the newspapers chose to make Lord Charles the hero of
the hour. Jack sighed. If only he could turn back the clock.
It was only such a short time ago that they had been
roistering together and he had basked in Lord Charles's
popularity. Lord Charles boxed and fenced well and was
an expert shot and a capital whip. When they were
friends, Jack had assumed these assets of personality and
skill to be his own. He blamed his present unpopularity
on the fact that Lord Charles had soured his soul, and his

lack of skill in every manly sport on the fact that Lord Charles had taken his confidence away. But more than anything did he blame Harriet Brown.

Many might think Harriet Brown, expensively gowned, to be a tolerably fine woman, but Jack damned her as a dowd. His idea of beauty was the beauty of the most luscious whores with their saucy dresses and highly painted faces and raucous laughter. To think that his friend had fallen for such as Harriet Brown proved the war must have addled his brains.

As he pondered the matter, Jack reflected on Lord Charles's dislike of whores. Now if he, Jack, could prove that this Miss Brown was whorish herself, then Charles would no longer continue to court her. Jack firmly believed in any case that all women were whores under the skin. He knew she was to attend the Raby's ball, as he himself had received an invitation and had gleaned that information from the secretary when he had called on the Marchioness of Raby personally to deliver his acceptance. He was also relieved that he had received the invitation, glad that all of society had not cut him off, and not knowing the Marchioness of Raby still believed him to be a friend of Lord Charles Marsham.

He decided to try to seduce Harriet Brown at the ball or do something that would make it look as if she had at least led him on.

A few streets away from him, another gentleman was wondering how to bring about the downfall of Harriet. Mr. Desmond Callaghan, the Tribbles' old enemy, thought that a disgraced Harriet would bring shame and distress on the Tribbles. But how was he to get close enough to her to effect that disgrace? He knew she was to attend the fancy dress ball, for he gossiped on the fringes of society and had learned the now famous Miss

Brown was to attend. He himself did not have an invitation, but he was an expert at getting into houses to which he had not been invited. He usually hovered outside until a large and distinguished group of guests arrived and attached himself to them and was usually accepted as being part of their party. Everyone had a guilty secret, thought Mr. Callaghan. Miss Brown was bound to have something in her past she did not want anyone to know about. He must get her to confide in him. But what woman at a ball was going to confide in a strange man?

His friend "Sniffy" Carpenter interrupted his worryings. Sniffy, so called because of his nervous habit of perpetually sniffing, was another beau of the demimonde, almost as foppishly dressed as Mr. Callaghan. He had heard a highly false account of how the Tribble sisters had stolen Mr. Callaghan's inheritance and, being of weak brain, encouraged his friend in all his plots and plans.

"So you see, Sniffy," said Mr. Callaghan, after he had outlined his vague plan. "I want to get her to confide in me, but I'm blessed if I know how to go about it."

"Pity you ain't a female," said Sniffy. "M'sister says females always chatter away at balls and talk scandal."

"That's it!" cried Mr. Callaghan. "I'll masquerade as a female. It's fancy dress."

Sniffy looked intrigued. "But will you be able to recognize her? They'll all be wearing masks."

"She's got masses of black hair, and most of the ladies have theirs cropped short. Besides, I've been watching the house, and that dressmaker, Yvette, has been coming and going. I paid a visit to her workshop, ostensibly to look for ideas for a costume for a lady friend who was going to the ball, and flattered her handiwork, so she showed me round her work-room, saying this costume was for Lady This and that costume for Lady That. So I picks up one at random and says, 'Is this for Miss Brown, the Tribbles' gal?' And she says, 'Oh, no, *this* is Miss Brown's costume,' and holds up some dreary Puritan outfit. So I shall go dressed the same and use that to enter into conversation."

He minced up and down the room and his voice rose to a high falsetto, "La, ma'am, we are gowned the same. I declare you must hate me."

Sniffy fell about laughing and said it was better than watching any play.

Jack Perkins, too, had finally thought of the problem of recognizing Harriet among so many costumed and masked people. To that end, he hung about Holles Street until he spotted a maidservant taking the air at the top of the area steps. He bribed her generously and so learned that Miss Brown was going in the dress of a Cromwellian maid.

That evening, Yvette tenderly wrapped Harriet's costume in tissue paper, told the nursery maid to take care of George, and set out to deliver it to Harriet. Yvette walked slowly towards Holles Street, thinking of the time she had lived there as the Tribbles' resident dressmaker. She knew neither of the sisters had quite forgiven her for leaving and setting up her own business, but did not know that it was her happy baby the Tribbles missed. Amy, in particular, had doted on George, imagining he would always be with them. She had chosen a school for him, then university, and then a fine regiment. Initially the sisters had been frequent visitors to Yvette's dressmaking business, but when they called, it was to find George enraptured by his nursery maid, a jolly young country girl, and indifferent to their presence, and so they had begun to feel unnecessary and unwanted.

Harriet was sitting in her bedchamber, ruefully surveying her new crop in the glass when Yvette entered. "I feel like a shorn lamb," she said over her shoulder. "But those abductors cut off such a hank of hair that Miss Amy said it would be better if I had it all short."

"It looks well," said Yvette, laying the costume on a chair and coming to stand behind her. Harriet's hair was curled all over her head. The effect was to make her look much younger and her blue eyes larger.

Harriet turned round in her chair and looked up at the dressmaker. "Yvette, do you ever think of that man, Monsieur Duclos?"

"Bien sûr," said Yvette with a shrug. "But what would you? He is gone and that is that."

"But if he ever came back . . . ?"

"He will not come back, Miss Brown. We are now at peace with France and he could have returned any time he chose. He did not choose. So I forget him as much as possible."

The door opened and Effy came in bearing a bouquet of flowers. "More flowers!" said Harriet as Effy laid the bouquet down on the chair on top of the costume. Amy appeared behind Effy in the doorway.

"I assume they are from Mr. Randolph," said Amy.

A flash of malice lit up Effy's eyes. Over the years, she could never understand why it was that Amy was usually the one favoured by the gentlemen. "Perhaps not," she said slyly. "Perhaps I have more than one admirer."

Amy snorted. "Like who?"

"Like Mr. Haddon."

Something snapped inside Amy. She was engulfed by such a wave of jealousy that Effy, Harriet, Yvette, and the flowers swam before her eyes in a red mist.

"A paltry offering," said Amy thinly, "and some of the flowers are faded already. They would be better on the fire." And before any of the others could stop her, she had seized up the bouquet, catching up the costume under-neath at the same time, and thrown the whole lot onto the fire, which was burning briskly.

"My flowers!" screamed Effy.

"My gown!" exclaimed Yvette. She seized the tongs and dragged the dress in its blazing tissue paper from the fire, but it continued to burn merrily. Harriet picked up a jug of water from the wash-stand and threw it over the gown.

"It is ruined," wailed Yvette. "How could you do such a thing, Miss Amy?"

"Yes, how could you," said Harriet severely. "You know those flowers were from Mr. Randolph. Miss Effy was simply teasing you."

"I don't care," said Amy, and slammed out of the room.

Amy went down to the drawing-room and sat beside the fire, her legs shaking. She wondered whether she was going mad.

But it was hard to bear, this courtship of Effy. Mr. Lawrence had abruptly ceased to call and, not knowing he had been ordered to drop the game by Lord Charles the minute Harriet had told him of the start of Effy's court-ship, Amy wondered and wondered if she had said any-thing to give him a disgust of her. Mr. Haddon called, of course, but the evenings were not the same. Now Mr. Randolph fussed over Effy and Mr. Haddon's normally polite and correct behaviour seemed chilly to Amy by comparison.

Amy thought miserably of her own atrocious behav-iour. She never knew where these rages came from, bring-ing with them headaches and an aching back. She would have to go and apologize, but perhaps it was better that Harriet would not be able to go in that severe costume.

She thought wearily of the long years of hopes and

dreams. She had believed when she was younger that age would bring resignation and calm, that the sexual fires would slowly burn away, and that she would become placid and serene. Her lined face and grey-streaked hair told her every day that youth was long past; but inside, she still felt like a young girl, so that her mirror image mocked her and silently cried out to her that her dreams were ridiculous and undignified.

She felt she could not bear one more ball or party. If only Harriet would wed just someone, anyone, then she would wait until Effy's marriage and then sell the house and retire to the country and become one of those crazy old spinsters.

Could she have guessed, Amy would have been vastly cheered to know that Mr. Lawrence was missing his visits. The gambling tables had lost of lot of their charm. Gambling meant drinking and smoking, and for the first time in his life he began to fret over days wasted in taking rhubarb-pills and drinking hock and seltzer in order to fortify himself for another evening ahead. The Tribbles were never boring. They seemed to lead highly adventurous lives. Amy's tough and agile mind, her occasional unmaidenly outbursts of swearing amused him. He had enjoyed sitting in their drawing-room among the feminine clutter. His nephew had told him the game was over, but surely there was no reason why he should not go on calling for his own sake. He knew they were to go to the costume ball. He would seek them out there and renew the friendship, and if Charles did not like it, then Charles could go to the devil.

On the afternoon of the day the ball was to be held, Lord Charles called on Harriet and heard the story of the ruined dress. "And I planned to go as a Cavalier to your Roundhead," he said. "Have you another costume?"

Harriet shook her head. "I am wearing a ball gown but I shall be masked, of course."

He leaned forward and lowered his voice so that the Tribble sisters, sitting at the other end of the drawing-room, should not hear. "And how go your plans for the Misses Tribble?"

"Mr. Randolph is courting Miss Effy most assiduously," whispered Harriet. "He sends flowers almost every day, but Mr. Haddon remains much the same, and that is upsetting poor Miss Amy, who feels left out of all the romance."

"Should you try so hard? She must have given up all thoughts of romance a long time ago."

Harriet gave an impatient cluck and, forgetting, raised her voice. "How can you be so blind?"

Amy watched the pair. She saw the way Lord Charles's handsome face was very close to Harriet's. His cat was lying on Harriet's lap, purring sleepily. She heard Harriet say, "How can you be so blind?" and stiffened with alarm. Harriet Brown was a very forthright girl. If Harriet had fallen in love with Lord Charles, then she would not hesitate to let him know it. And she must never do that, thought Amy. At the moment, Amy was sure, Harriet Brown was an amusing novelty to Lord Charles.

Now Lord Charles was leaning even closer, his voice a bare murmur in the quiet room. Harriet looked first startled and then gratified. What was that rake saying to her?

Lord Charles was explaining that he had received a letter from Monsieur Duclos, Yvette's faithless lover. "In so short a time!" exclaimed Harriet. "How can this be?"

"I forgot to tell you. A friend told me that the Comte De Ville was residing at an inn at Dover, having suffered dreadfully from mal de mer. So I sent an express there. Duclos said he would travel to London as soon as his old master had recovered."

"That is splendid news!" cried Harriet, and then her face fell. "It is not very lover-like, on the other hand. He should have set out immediately."

"He also says in his letter that he is afraid to face Yvette. He is sure she will never forgive him."

Harriet frowned. "You must write again and very quickly," she said after a short silence.

"And what would you like me to say?"

"You must say that he has to call here first and see me. For if he goes straight to Yvette, he will blurt out about the baby and that would never do."

"How so?"

"He must tell her he came expressly to see her, not because his master happened to be travelling to England."

"Have you not considered, Capability Brown, that Yvette might be better off without the scoundrel?"

"Yes, but I shall make up my mind about that when I see him."

"You should let me interview the fellow for you. You do not have much experience of men."

"I can tell bad from good."

"Then why do you give me the time of day?" he asked, his eyes teasing her.

"Because you are of use and you came to find me and rescue me and you are kind to the cat."

"Alas," he mourned. "That shall be my epitaph. 'Kind to cats.' "

He rose to take his leave. Amy followed him from the room and down the stairs. "I would like a word in private with you, Lord Charles," she said, and held open the door of the downstairs saloon.

"After you, Miss Amy," he said with a slight bow.

When they were seated, Amy looked at him seriously. She looked at his fine slim figure, small waist, good legs, and then at his handsome, clever face and those mocking green eyes, so like the cat, which had followed them in and now sat on the floor between them, looking from one face to the other.

"My lord," said Amy, "I must insist that your visits here cease."

The humour left Lord Charles's face. He raised his thin eyebrows and surveyed her haughtily and waited for her to continue.

"I think you must know why I ask. Miss Brown has been sent to us so that we may find her a suitable husband. To that end, I have asked Mr. Feathers to escort her to the ball. *He* is all that is suitable. I do not want false hopes raised in Harriet by your calls. Any gentleman interested in her, moreover, will be put off by your constant attendance on her. Do I make myself clear?"

"Yes, very clear, Miss Tribble," he said acidly. "And now, if you have quite finished, may I take my leave?"

"Oh, do not think too hardly of me," said Amy. "Harriet is a fine girl, very moral, very sound. I know she amuses you for the moment, but what is a mere amusement to you might be serious to her."

Lord Charles rose and bowed. He stooped and picked up the cat and tucked it under his arm.

"Good day to you, Miss Tribble," he said.

After he had gone, Amy felt very low. She had hoped he would protest that his intentions were honourable. But Harriet was at heart a sensible girl. She had accepted the fact that Mr. Feathers was to escort her without a murmur. He was a plain, boring man, but she had to marry someone, and a girl with a small dowry and aged twenty-five years could not hope to look any higher.

When Harriet saw Amy that evening, she wished she could have gone in costume herself. Amy made a magnificent Queen Elizabeth, complete with red wig and enormous ruff, and Effy was a dainty gypsy queen with a scarf embellished with gold coins on her head and a scarlet sash around her tiny waist. The effect was slightly spoiled by the fact that Effy had insisted on wearing blue muslin.

Mr. Haddon was in ordinary evening dress, but little Mr. Randolph had blossomed forth as the leader of a gypsy band, looking quite unlike himself with his face stained brown and a ferocious fake moustache. Mr. Feathers, having been told by Amy about Harriet's costume before it was ruined, was dressed as a Puritan.

Amy had been praying earnestly for charity and good will towards her sister. Why should not just the one of them find happiness? She was so intent on behaving herself that she barely seemed aware of Mr. Haddon.

Desmond Callaghan sat before a toilet-table in the room allocated to the ladies and studied his appearance in the glass with satisfaction. He was wearing a severe black gown with a white collar and on top of a wig of black glossy hair was perched a white bonnet. He adjusted his black velvet mask. He was still glowing from his friend Sniffy's praise. The feminine streak in him delighted in the masquerade and he was inclined to think he looked a much finer figure of a woman than most of the ladies about him.

He gave a final pat to his wig and then made his way up to the ballroom. "Name please?" said the major-domo. Mr. Callaghan thought quickly. He dare not give a strange false name and so alert the marchioness to the fact that there was a gatecrasher at her ball, and so he said calmly, "Miss Harriet Brown."

For a brief moment a flicker of surprise showed in the major-domo's eyes. He had already introduced a Miss Harriet Brown. But it was a common-enough name, and so in stentorian tones he announced Mr. Callaghan. Jack Perkins, who had arrived just after the real Harriet, looked up. Jealousy had made him remember Harriet as a plain frump and this awful simpering creature was every bit as horrible as his imaginings. With a triumphant smile, he headed towards her. Two elderly dowagers had made their entrance just behind Mr. Callaghan, and so he assumed they were the Tribble sisters; as on the night he had first seen Harriet he had been too interested in trying to get a good look at her to take much notice of her companions.

Mr. Haddon did not feel like dancing. He had decided to sit beside Amy and chat and leave the dancing to the others. To his annoyance, no sooner had he seated himself beside Amy than a vaguely familiar figure dressed as Sir Walter Raleigh and wearing a blue velvet mask bowed before Amy and asked for the pleasure of the first waltz.

"Mr. Lawrence!" cried Amy, her quick eyes recognizing the old gambler under the fancy dress and mask. "How clever of you."

Mr. Lawrence smiled. "We make the perfect pair." Mr. Haddon was left alone to watch the couple dancing. How elegantly Amy moved! Her eyes glittered wickedly behind her mask at something Mr. Lawrence was saying.

Harriet, waltzing with Mr. Feathers, who kept stepping

on her toes with his thick Cromwellian boots, saw Lord Charles entering the ballroom. He was dressed as a Cavalier in blue silk and lace. On his arm, attired as a fairy queen, was Lisa Seymour. They seemed well pleased with each other's company.

And why should I mind? Harriet chided herself. I introduced them.

Mr. Desmond Callaghan was circulating in the arms of Jack Perkins. Jack was paying him very warm compliments and Mr. Callaghan maliciously saved each one up in his mind to relate to an admiring Sniffy. His eyes searched the ballroom but he could not see another Puritan maid. He would have guessed the identity of Harriet if he could have recognized the Tribble sisters, but hard as he looked, he did not spot the handsome red-wigged Queen Elizabeth as Amy, or the small, dainty gypsy queen with a gold mask as Effy.

The garden outside the ballroom had been covered over by an enormous marquee for the evening, and tubs of trees and hothouse flowers lined the walks to create the illusion of a garden in summer. Paper leaves and lanterns decorated the bare branches of the winter trees.

Jack thought quickly. If he could get "Harriet" out there, he might be able to have a go at her, as he described it to himself. He was convinced he was a success with the ladies, simply because the whores he paid for their attentions were good at their job and knew how to flatter and tease as part of their trade. Top prostitutes knew the competition was fierce in an overcrowded market and that they had to supply more than bare sex; they had to master the arts of how to charm and entertain as well. But Jack put it all down to his own irresistible attractions. He decided it would be better if he tried to get his lady tipsy first.

As the waltz came to an end, he said, "What about some champagne, my fair one?"

Mr. Callaghan glanced towards the side room where refreshments were being served. Perhaps Harriet was there. Besides, he longed for a drink.

"Thank you, kind sir," he said in a high falsetto.

Soon they were sharing a bottle of champagne, and then another. Jack Perkins was cursing this hard-headed woman who seemed able to sink glass after glass without it having any visible effect.

But unknown to him, his partner was becoming tipsy, and the more tipsy he became, the more Mr. Callaghan began to enjoy the situation. He was determined to lead Jack on, simply to furnish wide-eyed and admiring Sniffy with the best story he had ever heard.

After the third bottle of champagne, Jack suggested thickly they take a stroll in the gardens. The gardens! That was where she might be, thought Mr. Callaghan woozily. He rapped Jack on the arm with his fan and said flirtatiously, "La, sir. I hope you will behave yourself."

"I will try to restrain myself," said Jack, propelling Mr. Callaghan towards the garden. He noticed there were dark walks and secluded arbours. He marched Mr. Callaghan in the direction of one of these arbours made from potted plants.

Mr. Callaghan sat down, adjusted his mask, and lowered his eyes modestly. Jack sank on one knee in front of him and grasped his gloved hand.

"Fair one," he breathed. "You set my senses reeling."

Mr. Callaghan stifled a laugh and said, "Naughty! You are become too warm."

"It is my passion for you," said Jack. "A kiss is all I ask."

Suddenly sobered, Mr. Callaghan rose to his feet and backed away. "I am going to the ballroom," he said firmly.

Jack leaped up and seized Mr. Callaghan around the waist.

They were now out of the arbour and in full view of the ballroom. The dance had finished and the guests began to stare at the couple.

"Leave me alone, damn you," muttered Mr. Callaghan, trying to wrench himself free.

"So you want my leg across you," shouted Jack, sure that he was ruining the reputation of Harriet Brown. "Then, demme, you shall have it!"

"Let me go!" shouted Mr. Callaghan. He struck Jack across the face.

Jack tore off Mr. Callaghan's mask, determined that everyone should see it was Harriet Brown. Mr. Callaghan reeled backwards and his wig and bonnet went flying.

Amy Tribble's voice, loud with amazement, sounded from the ballroom like a clarion call. "Good heavens! It's that dreadful Mr. Callaghan masquerading as a woman, with some fellow trying to seduce him."

White with fury, the Marchioness of Raby was calling to her servants to throw the pair out. Lord Charles walked up to where Jack stood, gazing in horror at Mr. Callaghan.

"You fool, Jack," he said. "From the costume that creature is wearing, I have the mad idea you thought that was Harriet Brown and planned to ruin her."

"It's all your fault," howled Jack, and he was still howling threats and accusations as he and Mr. Callaghan were bundled out into the street together.

Jack swung round on Mr. Callaghan. "You backgammon player," he said.

"How dare you call me a homosexual," raged Mr. Callaghan, close to tears. "I demand satisfaction."

"And you shall have it," growled Jack. "Here is my card. Send your seconds to see me in the morning."

Mr. Callaghan was suddenly aware of the laughing, jeering faces about him as coachmen and grooms gathered to look at this man in woman's clothes. He ran off down the street, bolting towards his lodgings like a hunted animal.

Lord Charles was worried. Harriet was still surrounded by threats, and Amy Tribble had ordered him to leave her alone. But who else was capable of looking after her? Not that idiot, Feathers. It was not Harriet's bosom in which he had raised false hopes, but that of that tiresome creature, Lisa Seymour. Did Harriet think so very little of him that she should consider such a female good enough for him?

But he was still hurt and furious at Amy and did not go near Harriet. Instead, he asked Lisa Seymour for another dance, hoping Harriet would notice, and then, after he had asked Lisa, wondering at his own childish behaviour.

Meanwhile, the Marchioness of Raby, recovered from her shock, took Mr. Feathers aside and commanded him "to get on with it," meaning to propose to Harriet Brown. So Mr. Feathers dutifully asked Harriet to walk with him in the garden.

Harriet had noticed Lord Charles and Lisa. It was a lively country dance and they seemed to be enjoying themselves. She sadly allowed Mr. Feathers to lead her into the garden. He would propose, she would accept. He had a very thin neck, she noticed, and a prominent Adam's apple. She tried to console herself with the thought of children and what a comfort they would be in a loveless marriage, but all she could think of was a brood of little boys in Puritan dress with thin necks. Her eyes filled with tears and she blinked them away.

Lord Charles was crossing hands with Lisa to go down

the middle of the dance when he saw Harriet Brown sitting in the garden, with Mr. Feathers getting down on his knees in front of her. Lisa laughed, as, instead of letting her hands go at the bottom of the dance, Lord Charles kept firmly hold of them and danced her into the garden and right up to Mr. Feathers. Blushing under his mask, Mr. Feathers got to his feet.

The laughter died on Lisa's lips. Lord Charles was looking earnestly at Harriet and she was looking back at him. Neither Lisa nor Mr. Feathers appeared to exist for the couple.

"My lord," protested Lisa sharply, "we have left the dance and you are interrupting a courtship."

"Nonsense," said Lord Charles. "I am sure Mr. Feathers was simply stooping to tie his lace."

"Yes, that was it," said Mr. Feathers, too embarrassed to admit he had been trying to propose marriage while Lisa looked scornfully down at his laceless boots.

The last chord of the music died away and a gong sounded. "Supper," cried Lord Charles. "Miss Seymour, I must beg you to excuse me. Miss Brown is engaged to take supper with me. Perhaps Mr. Feathers . . . ?"

Lisa's face under her mask coloured up with fury. Without a word she turned on her heel and walked away. Lord Charles held out his arm to Harriet. "May I have the honour of escorting you, Miss Brown?"

For a bare moment, Harriet hesitated. She should tell him to go to the devil, sit down again, and accept her future with Mr. Feathers. But somehow she found herself rising and taking his arm and curtsying to Mr. Feathers and murmuring an apology.

Mr. Feathers watched her go with relief. He had tried and he had failed through no fault of his own. Now he could enjoy the ball.

"That was bad of you," said Harriet quietly when they were seated. "Very bad."

"He is not for you, Miss Brown. You didn't want him. Admit the truth."

"No, I didn't want him," sighed Harriet. "But I must settle for someone."

"True. But not him. You would not be happy."

Harriet looked at him impatiently. "Quite a lot of us on this earth cannot have everything we want. Very few of us are rich enough to pick and choose."

She bent her head and he looked at her with compassion. "Miss Brown . . . Harriet," he said urgently. "I have a suggestion, a proposition to make to you."

Harriet looked at him steadily. A little while ago she had been in despair. Now she felt she was in heaven.

"Go on," she said softly.

"I am a rich man. I will furnish you with a large sum of money. In that way, you will have a good dowry, which means you may have your pick; and if you do not wish to marry, why, you may still have the money to support yourself."

Harriet quickly lowered her eyes and sat very still. She was disappointed. She thought he had been going to propose. She must feel so terribly disappointed because London had made her worldly and sinful and she was yearning after a title.

"It is a generous offer," she said stiffly, "but I cannot accept it."

"Why not?"

"I am quite old and well able to take care of myself. I am sensible enough to settle for some man or other, probably Mr. Feathers, and accept my lot. There is strength in humility, Lord Charles."

"There he is again," said Amy crossly to Mr. Haddon.

The sight of that trouble-maker, Mr. Callaghan, had brought them together.

Mr. Haddon raised his quizzing-glass and studied Lord Charles and Harriet.

"I think he is falling in love with her," he said.

"How would *you* know," retorted Miss Amy Tribble crossly. "You wouldn't know love if you met it in your soup."

"What gives you that impression?"

"Because you're a dry old stick," said Amy furiously.

He gave her an amazed, hurt look and turned his shoulder on her and began to talk to the lady on his other side. Mr. Lawrence, who was on the other side of Amy, eagerly seized the chance to engage her in conversation. Mr. Lawrence had made up his mind to court Amy. Periodically, during his life, he had decided to marry, going so far as to propose on two occasions and then having to get himself out of it when he came to the inevitable conclusion that he preferred his quiet hedonistic life. He sensed competition from Mr. Haddon and that added spice and impetus to the chase. He helped her to food and more wine and flattered her appearance until Amy began to glow and feel young again.

After supper, he asked her to walk with him in the garden and Amy dreamily agreed. Mr. Haddon watched them go. He feared for Amy. He did not trust Lawrence one bit. He reflected sourly that Amy was as naive as a schoolgirl and not able to take care of herself.

In the garden, Mr. Lawrence plucked a flower and handed it to Amy. He looked about. The gardens were quiet. First he would steal a kiss, then he would propose. Amy saw his lips approaching hers and closed her eyes and trembled. Amy Tribble had never been kissed before.

His lips descended on her own and Amy felt . . . nothing. She knew in that instant that the only man in the whole of the world she wanted to kiss her was Mr. Haddon. She drew away gently from Mr. Lawrence, tears sparkling in her eyes.

Mr. Haddon had walked into the garden just in time to witness that kiss. He was possessed of a cold fury. He saw the tears in Amy's eyes and that was enough for him.

He marched up to Mr. Lawrence and struck him across the face with his gloves and then threw them on the grass. "You old charlatan," said Mr. Haddon. "I demand satisfaction." He waited for Mr. Lawrence to pick up the gloves and so accept his challenge.

Another scene. Harriet, who was just being returned to the ballroom by Lord Charles, stood beside him and watched the tableau in the garden.

Mr. Lawrence looked down at the gloves lying on the grass, but he did not stoop to pick them up. He felt weary and old and wondered if he had run mad. All he wanted now was the comfort of his lodgings and the old tranquillity of his usual life. Then he looked up and saw Lord Charles.

"Nephew!" he cried.

Lord Charles walked quickly up to him, followed by Harriet.

"This fellow has challenged me to a duel and all because I kissed Miss Amy," said Mr. Lawrence. "But she let me kiss her."

"And so I did," said Amy quietly.

"My uncle is not fighting any duel, Mr. Haddon," said Lord Charles. "You misunderstood the situation. Take Miss Amy inside and have something cooling to drink."

"Please," whispered Amy brokenly.

Mr. Haddon bent down and picked up his gloves. He held out his arm to Amy and walked slowly off with her.

"Thank you, dear boy," sighed Mr. Lawrence. "I am too old for pistols at dawn. I shall go home now and lie down. I have had a bad shock."

"There you are, Capability Brown," said Lord Charles, watching him go. "By that one kiss, I feel he has done a lot to further matters between Miss Amy and Mr. Haddon."

"But to kiss Miss Amy! That was vastly shocking."

"It was only a kiss. What's in a kiss?"

"I forget your years of experience, my lord," said Harriet crossly. "I would not accept a kiss lightly."

"You may have to accept kisses and deeper intimacies you do not like, Harriet Brown. Think you of lying in Mr. Feather's bed and Mr. Feather's arms?"

"You disgusting rake," said Harriet, overwrought by all the see-sawing emotions of the evening. "I saw you kissing those whores outside the Argyle Rooms with your dirty soiled lips."

"Lips," he said, suddenly furious, "which you would never allow to sully your own."

"Exactly, Lord Charles Marsham."

Her bosom was heaving and her eyes were glittering behind her mask. An errant draught whistled through the lamps above their head and blew them out, plunging the pair into shadow.

He jerked her into his arms and kissed her hard. Shock and amazement kept her rigid in his arms. And then her body was racked with such searing passion that she thought she would faint. For one brief heady moment she responded to him and then, in the next moment, she tore herself away, scrubbing at her lips with the back of her glove and looking at him with hurt eyes. Then she turned about and walked away. She knew why her body had behaved so disgustingly and wantonly. It was because he was experienced at making love to women and knew, no doubt, exactly how to rouse their passions.

Lord Charles watched her go, amazement on his face. He could still feel the sweetness of her lips and his body ached and throbbed with a sudden yearning for her.

He went into the ballroom and then into the refreshment room, where Amy and Mr. Haddon were sitting side by side.

"Miss Tribble," said Lord Charles. "I beg your permission to call on you tomorrow. I have something to ask you."

"By all means," said Amy quietly. "What time?"

"Ten o'clock."

"Much too early. Say about two?"

"Thank you," said Lord Charles. He bowed and turned away.

Amy let out a long breath. "Another success, or I'm not mistaken," she said triumphantly. "He loves her after all. Oh, thank God. It is such a strain, the work and worry of finding mates for these girls. Ah, well, I had hoped that would be the last, but I suppose we had better face up to another Season."

"And more frights and more adventures?" pointed out Mr. Haddon.

"Oh, we have been unlucky in that respect. It can't go on like this. Makes me feel old."

"I don't think you will ever be old, Miss Amy. Allowing yourself to be kissed in the garden, indeed!"

"That was the first time I had ever been kissed," said Amy ruefully. "It was not what I expected. That was why I felt like crying."

"You should not have allowed yourself to be kissed in the first place."

Amy's temper snapped. "You pompous dried-up stick

with iced water in your veins," she said. "What can you know of love or passion, something you have never known? Oh, I am sorry, Mr. Haddon. I do not know why I am so rude to you."

Mr. Haddon looked about the supper-room. It was deserted except for the pair of them. The jaunty strains of a Scotch reel filtered into the room. He leaned forward and untied the strings of Amy's mask and removed it. Her plain honest face looked back at him in amazement. Then he gathered her to him and kissed her very tenderly. Amy's heart rose to her lips and she kissed him back with all the sincerity and passion and honesty in her soul.

"Oh, Amy," said Mr. Haddon at last. He was breathing raggedly and two spots of colour burned on his cheeks. "Will you do me the honour, the very great honour of . . . ?"

"Yes," said Amy Tribble. "Oh, my stars and garters. Yes!"

Effy Tribble lay back on her lacy pillow that night, a smile of satisfaction on her lips. Mr. Randolph had paid her every compliment, every attention. She hoped Amy would look in before she went to sleep, so that she could afford herself the luxury of telling her about it. Poor Amy. When she, Effy, was married to Mr. Randolph, she would try to visit Amy as often as possible and to be very, very kind. She would persuade Mr. Randolph to give Amy a pension so that Amy would not need to go on working any more. Of course, it was hard on Amy that Effy should marry, but Effy reflected that it was time her sister realized that she was downright plain by comparison. Effy raised her hand mirror from the bedside table and surveyed herself complacently in the glass.

And then Amy walked in and sat down on the bed with a dreamy smile on her face.

"You've been drinking too much," said Effy sharply, and then softened her voice, because poor Amy was much to be pitied.

Then Harriet walked in as well and said, "Miss Amy, would you like me to go down to the kitchens and fetch you a glass of hot milk? That was a shocking affair this evening."

"What affair?" demanded Effy.

"Oh, did you not hear?" exclaimed Harriet. "I thought everyone knew about it. Mr. Lawrence took Miss Amy into the garden and kissed her and Mr. Haddon challenged him to a duel, but Lord Charles interceded and all was settled amicably enough." Then Harriet looked in surprise at Effy. Her normally pretty face had turned sour and old.

Then Effy smiled and laughed. "That old roué. He would kiss anyone. I'm surprised at you, Amy. No doubt Mr. Haddon delivered himself of a jaw-me-dead." Effy's face became mock-serious. She was soon to be a matron and looked forward to lecturing Amy from the height of her married status. It would do no harm to impart words of wisdom to her sister now. "You must realize, Amy dear, that gentlemen such as Mr. Haddon cannot be made jealous, if such was your intention."

"It wasn't," said Amy with a dreamy, reminiscent smile, "but he was."

"You are fantasizing again, sister."

"And when he kissed me and asked me to marry him, I thought I would die from happiness."

"Oh, Miss Amy!" cried Harriet, her eyes like stars. "I wish you all the happiness in the world."

"What . . . did . . . you . . . say?" demanded Effy in a

harsh, grating voice, quite unlike her usual cooing tones.

"I'm to be married," said Amy. "Mr. Haddon wants us to be married as soon as possible."

Effy began to cry.

"Dear sister," said Amy, "I knew you would share my happiness." And only the shrewd Harriet Brown noticed that Miss Effy was crying with rage.

Chapter 7

Far in the stillness
A cat languishes loudly.
—William Ernest Henley

MR. CALLAGHAN PACKED hurriedly next day. This time it was not only fear of a duel that drove him to flight but the terror of ridicule. The newspapers had got hold of the story of his impersonation of a woman and his attempted seduction by Jack Perkins. He thought tearfully that such an aristocrat as the Marchioness of Raby ought to have known how to hush such things up and wondered how the newspapers had managed to discover his name, not knowing that the marchioness herself had sent an account to the press, well aware that any successful hostess could only increase her standing by having a good scandal at one of her receptions.

He was determined to find a ship and sail anywhere he could get a passage, somewhere to a kinder climate and kinder people. He thought the Tribbles must be witches, causing the humiliation and downfall of any who tried to harm them.

And so, when Jack Perkins came looking for him, Mr. Callaghan was well on his road to Bristol. Balked of his prey, Jack was determined on some sort of revenge. He, too, could not bear to remain in Town much longer, where he knew he would be subjected to jeers and taunts. If he could harm or upset Lord Charles in some way, then what caused pain to Lord Charles would also cause pain to that strumpet who had changed him from an easygoing friend into an enemy. Then he remembered the cat.

In all the euphoria of that proposal of marriage, Amy had forgotten to tell Harriet about Lord Charles's call. And so Harriet, who was studying her Italian grammar in her room, was surprised when Amy, much flustered, appeared to tell her that Lord Charles was downstairs in the saloon and anxious to speak to her.

"In the saloon? On the ground floor?" asked Harriet, surprised.

"Yes, he wishes to be private with you, if you take my meaning."

Harriet looked blank. Amy opened her mouth to say he had come to propose, and then decided against it. Why raise the girl's hopes only to find out afterwards that Lord Charles had only called to say the cat was sick, or some such rubbish like that.

"Change your gown," urged Amy. "Put on the pretty blue one."

Harriet coloured as she remembered that kiss and her

unmaidenly reaction. "My old gown will do very well," she said quietly.

She made her way down to the ground floor, one hand lingering on the banister, her steps slow. She was disappointed in Lord Charles. Kisses should be sweet and chaste, inspiring a sort of spiritual glow, not wanton, lustful urges. Her father's favourite sermon had been the one about the lusts of the flesh. She must thank Lord Charles for all he had done to help the Tribble sisters and then suggest that they should not meet again.

A dismal and familiar feeling of martyrdom came over her, for she had given up many childhood delights and treats at her father's request because "such sacrifice is good for you."

Lord Charles stopped pacing the room as she entered. He looked very elegant and very charming. He gave her a fleeting smile and then gazed at her seriously and said, "Well, Miss Brown?"

"Well, what, my lord?" asked Harriet.

"Did not Miss Amy warn you? I am here to ask you to marry me."

Harriet raised her hands to her face and looked at him in dismay. Everyone knew that ladies had souls above lust and passion, common women did not. He must feel he had compromised her in some way, so ran Harriet's mad thoughts.

She lowered her hands and said firmly, "It is not necessary, my lord. No, not at all. You must not blame yourself."

"For what?"

"For kissing me so wantonly."

"I agree with you I should have asked for permission to pay my addresses to you before I kissed you, but good heavens, my sweeting, what's in a kiss?"

Harriet shuddered. The correct answer to that was a world of passion and lust and yearning.

"Please go away," she said in a stifled voice. "It would be better, my lord, if you did not call on me again."

He moved towards her. "Harriet! Harriet, what are you talking about?"

"Don't touch me!" said Harriet with such a look of revulsion in her face that he was stopped in his tracks.

"I have given you a disgust of me," he said sadly. "Very well, Miss Brown. I see it is impossible to pursue the matter any further."

"Very sorry," whispered Harriet brokenly and ran from the room, nearly colliding with Amy, who had been trying to listen from the hall.

Amy watched as Harriet ran up the stairs, her shoulders hunched. Then she went slowly into the saloon.

Lord Charles was drawing on his gloves.

"She doesn't like me a bit," he said bleakly.

"What did you do or say to frighten her?" asked Amy.

"Nothing. Well, I did behave a little boldly at the ball. I kissed her. She said I had kissed her wantonly, whatever that means."

"I will try to find out," said Amy.

"Do not waste your time." Lord Charles was becoming angry. "I made a mistake. I hope you find someone boring and dull enough to suit her Methodist tastes."

He bowed and Amy reluctantly curtsied and stood aside to let him pass.

She sat down, wondering what had gone wrong and then decided that she and Effy had blithely assumed that Lord Charles had only to want to marry Harriet for Harriet to want to marry him. It now seemed they had been mistaken. A little of her pleasure in her own engagement was dimmed. Now what were they going to do with Harriet?

While she was still sitting there worrying, Harris came in and said in startled tones, "That Frenchie's turned up and is asking for Miss Brown. He says he called earlier on Lord Charles and Lord Charles instructed him to come here."

"What Frenchie?" asked Amy, her hand to her brow.

"Monsoor Duclos. Erm, the one Ma'm'selle Yvette . . ." His voice trailed away.

Amy started to her feet, her face grim. "Send him in," she said coldly.

The former French tutor was ushered into the saloon. "How dare you show your face here?" demanded Amy.

Monsieur Duclos backed slightly before the fury on her face. "I had a letter from Lord Charles Marsham telling me about my son," he said. "I called on him and he said that I must first call on a Miss Brown."

"Miss Brown is not able to see you," retorted Amy harshly. Then the door opened and Harriet walked in. She had been descending the stairs to tell Amy about the proposal when she met the butler, who had informed her about the arrival of the Frenchman. She was at first puzzled that Lord Charles's letter telling Monsieur Duclos to call on her first should have reached him so quickly until Harris explained the Frenchman had been first to see Lord Charles and Lord Charles had instructed him to see Miss Brown.

"It is all right, Miss Amy," said Harriet quietly. "Monsieur Duclos is here on my instructions, and what I have to say to him is private."

Amy opened her mouth to protest, but there was a sad dignity about Harriet that stopped the words. She reluctantly left the pair together.

"Now, Monsieur Duclos," said Harriet when they were alone, "I asked you to call here first because I wish to warn you not to tell Yvette that you know she has borne you a son."

"But why?"

"First, I must ask your intentions."

"To marry her."

"And only because of the boy?"

"No, not that," said Monsieur Duclos wretchedly. "I have thought of nothing but her. I have saved and saved so that we might marry. I at last told my employer and he said he would allow me to marry, but I must wait until he was ready to return to England."

"You must tell Yvette it is because of your love for her that you have returned," said Harriet, "and do not let it appear that you simply want your son. You will have a difficult enough time as it is."

He broke into rapid French and Harriet shook her head in dismay. All those French lessons and she could not make out a single word!

He reverted to English. "Please, miss," he begged, "bring her to me." He held out the letter from Lord Charles. Harriet miserably noted Lord Charles's address on the top of the paper and fought down a longing to run to him immediately and beg his forgiveness and say she would marry him. "Please let me see her," she realized Monsieur Duclos was saying.

"She no longer lives here," said Harriet. "She has her own dressmaking business."

Harriet turned Lord Charles's letter over and wrote the address of Yvette's business on the back.

Monsieur Duclos thanked her profusely.

Amy was waiting in the drawing-room when Harriet wearily mounted the stairs again.

"Come in here, child," she called, "and tell me about it."

"Monsieur Duclos . . ." began Harriet.

"I am not interested in that frog mountebank," snapped Amy, "except to hope that Yvette gives him the telling-off he deserves. What happened between you and Lord Charles? I should have warned you he was to call, but my own happiness put it out of my head."

"I could not marry him," said Harriet, hanging her head. "He does not make me feel like a lady."

"He was arrogant? Insulting? Sneered at your low background and lack of money?"

"None of these things. It was what happened when he kissed me."

Various lurid thoughts about ways of kissing rampaged through Amy's brain.

"You will need to explain."

"He is so experienced in making love to women," said Harriet, turning paler, "that a wanton reaction to his touch was set up in my body. Lust is what I am talking of, Miss Amy, and no lady feels lust."

"Oh, I see," said Amy, letting out a slow breath of relief. "Come and sit down next to me, Harriet. It is assumed, you see, that women do not have the passions of men. That is because in the masculine mind, passion suggests experience. A virgin is ideally supposed to be trembling and shy and submissive. The result is that a deal of unfortunate ladies remain like that during marriage, even though they beget a string of children, and so the men take their pleasures outside the marriage bed. But true love, Harriet, is a mixture of the sacred and the profane. Lord Charles's experience did not conjure up your response. Your love for him did, and there is nothing dirty or wrong about that. I was kissed by Mr. Lawrence, who is, if you like, an experienced old rip—the first time I had been kissed, too—and I felt nothing. But"—Amy closed her eyes—"when Mr. Haddon kissed me, I could have gone to hell and back for him. My soul and my body were on my lips. Do I make myself clear? Lord Charles, were he only interested in lust, could have any woman he wanted. But he wants you. And he must be very deeply in love to propose to a Methodist," pointed out Amy.

For one moment Amy's lined and plain face seemed to fade and it appeared to Harriet as if an eager young girl, full of passion and youth, sat facing her.

"What shall I do?" she asked.

"Follow your heart," said Amy. "I think you can still get him back. Sit down over there and write him a letter."

Jack Perkins was ushered into the library in Lord Charles's town house. Lord Charles had not bothered to inform his servants that Mr. Perkins was no longer welcome. Jack had lurked outside until he had seen Lord Charles leave. "I shall wait," he told the butler airily. "Taken that cat with him, I suppose?"

"No, sir. It is sleeping over there in the corner."

The cat, Tom, had eaten a large meal and appeared dead to the world.

"Well, fetch me a bottle of burgundy and I shall await your master's return," said Jack loftily.

He waited until the butler had left and rose slowly to his feet. In his hand he held a leather bag with a drawstring neck.

He inched cautiously towards the sleeping cat and then, quick as a flash, he stooped and seized Tom by the scruff of the neck and thrust him into the bag and tied the strings tight.

He made his way out of the library and quietly let himself out into the street and set off at an easy pace.

Inside the bag, Tom struggled and miaowed dismally.

Miss Harriet Brown, descending from a hired hack, heard that miaow. She recognized Jack Perkins and saw the bag in his hand from which the cries were coming. Harriet had decided to call on Lord Charles. She had not told Amy that she suddenly could not bear to sit quietly at home and wait for him to call on her.

The terrible thought crossed her mind that a rejected Lord Charles had asked this peculiar man to get rid of the cat for him. On the other hand, Jack Perkins could simply be taking the cat to Lord Charles, although carrying it in a bag was an odd way of doing it.

Harriet knocked furiously at the door of Lord Charles's town house, only to be told that the master was not at home.

She hurried down the steps and set out after Jack.

She followed him down St. James's Street, oblivious to the jeers and insults and catcalls that followed her, for no lady was ever supposed to walk down St. James's Street, then along Pall Mall, through Charing Cross, and so down Whitehall.

Lord Charles had been sitting at the bay window of White's as Jack Perkins went past. He saw him and was surprised his ex-friend had the nerve to remain in London. Then he idly watched a female hurrying along. She was dressed like a lady, in a merino wool cloak and close bonnet. He thought she looked like Harriet and then reflected cynically that the prim and correct Miss Brown would not be seen dead in St. James's Street.

His friend, Guy Sutherland, strolled up to join him.

"Saw that dreadful fellow, Perkins," said Guy. "Surprised he's still in Town."

"Hide like an ox," drawled Lord Charles indifferently.

"Must have had kittens. I mean, literally, the yowls coming from that bag he was carrying would wake the dead."

Lord Charles started to his feet. He remembered Jack's hatred of the cat and Jack was carrying a bag with a cat or cats in it.

Pushing past his startled friend, he ran from the club and set out in pursuit. If Jack meant to get rid of a cat, then Jack must have been bound for the river.

Tired and anxious, Harriet hurried on after Jack. She saw him heading for Westminster Bridge. Surely he must be going to meet Lord Charles. He could not possibly . . . She would not allow herself to finish the thought.

On he went, out into the middle of the bridge and into one of the bays, Harriet following.

He held the bag out over the river.

Harriet screamed, "Stop!"

Jack turned and saw her. His face creased in a smile of pure malice. He opened his hand and let the bag drop.

Harriet tore off her bonnet and cloak and dropped them to the ground and kicked off her half-boots. She climbed up onto the top of the parapet. Behind her, she could hear shouts and people running. She raised her hands above her head and dived.

Now, one of the delights of Scarborough that her strict father had not set his face against was swimming, and Harriet was a very powerful swimmer.

But for a long, black, nightmare time, she thought she would never reach the surface again after that dive. When her head at last rose above the River Thames, she shook the water from her eyes and looked desperately about her as she trod water.

The air inside the tough leather bag had made it act like

a balloon, cushioning the cat's fall and making the bag float on the water. As Harriet looked, she saw it being carried off downstream on a strong current. The water was icy and her skirts were dragging at her legs, but she set out in pursuit.

Jack Perkins saw Lord Charles running onto the bridge and took to his heels and fled.

And then Lord Charles heard a woman shout, "A suicide. Pore woman jist jumped in."

He leaned over in time to see Harriet surface and look about her. He shouted her name but she did not hear.

He threw his hat, coat, and cane on the ground and pulled off his boots, and, like Harriet, mounted the balustrade of the bay and dived in.

Harriet reached the bag and grasped hold of it. She tried to swim to the shore, but she was exhausted and the current was too strong. She floated on her back, clutching the bag on her chest, staring at the sky and noticing with a dazed wonder that large snowflakes were beginning to fall.

Then she heard a splashing beside her and struggled to see what it was. It was the face of Lord Charles Marsham.

"Don't talk," he shouted. "Tie the bag round my neck if you can and hang on to my shoulders."

Wearily and numbly, Harriet did as she was bid.

Fighting against the current, Lord Charles headed slowly to the Chelsea shore. They had been spotted and fishermen left their nets to wade out and help them. The snow was falling more thickly as they struggled up the narrow Chelsea beach. Through the swirling snow and across the meadows, Lord Charles could see the lights of the World's End public house.

"Help me get this lady to the pub," he said. The fishermen gathered around and produced a handcart. Harriet was put on the cart and the procession started towards the pub. "I am frightened to open this bag," said Harriet weakly. "Poor Tom is probably dead."

"More than likely," replied Lord Charles grimly. "Don't try to talk, Harriet, until we have you safe."

Harriet thought she would never forget the joy and relief of being ushered into that warm pub and of being taken upstairs to a bedchamber with a roaring fire. She knelt down beside the fire and laid the leather bag tenderly on the floor. Slowly she drew open the strings. Two furious green eyes stared out at her and then the cat emerged, unhurt, turned its back on her and began to wash its fur.

Lord Charles came in with an armful of clothes and dry towels to find Harriet on her knees, weeping over an indifferent cat.

"Forget about the cat and dry yourself," he said crossly. "Here, get into these clothes after you have dried yourself. I shall be back shortly. Come, Tom."

The cat followed him from the room like a dog.

Harriet stripped off her clothes, washed herself, towelled herself dry, and put on the faded, yellowing underwear and plain old-fashioned woollen dress someone at the inn had supplied. She was sitting at the toilet-table, brushing her hair, when Lord Charles came in. He was wearing old-fashioned knee-breeches, thick stockings, and heavy shoes, a cotton shirt, and a woollen jacket.

"What a pair of peasants we look," he said with a grin. "I have ordered a carriage for half an hour's time. You will soon be home."

A waiter entered carrying a decanter of brandy and two glasses. "Drink up," ordered Lord Charles after the waiter had left.

Harriet sipped at a glass of brandy and smiled at him sleepily.

146

He sat down on the bed and looked at her thoughtfully. "How did you come so opportunely to rescue the cat?" he asked.

"I was calling at your house and saw Jack Perkins leave. I heard the miaows from the bag and thought he might be taking the cat to you, so I followed him."

"And Capability Brown can of course swim like a fish. Why were you coming to see me?"

Harriet hung her head. "My reaction to your kiss frightened me," she said. "But Miss Amy . . ." Harriet closed her eyes and prayed for courage. "Miss Amy told me that I had reacted so . . . strongly . . . because, because I was . . . I am . . . in love with you."

"Was there ever such a school for manners!" said Lord Charles. "Come here to me, Harriet." She rose and stood shyly beside him.

He pulled her down onto the bed beside him and put an arm about her shoulders. "I think, you know," he said seriously, "that I should kiss you again just to make sure."

"Very well," said Harriet bravely, shutting her eyes tight and puckering up her lips. He laughed against her mouth. "Oh, my brave Methodist," he said and then his lips met hers in a long, drugging kiss. For one brief panic-stricken moment, Harriet thought her reaction this time was even more shocking than the last, but Amy Tribble had told her it was natural and right and Amy was a good woman.

She surrendered herself up to a world of different kisses—passionate, tender, loving, and then more passionate—until she was dizzy with emotion and thought in a dazed way she would never forget this room, or the smells of brandy and lavender and wood-smoke, or the altered, tender look on his face as he said, "You *will* marry me, my Harriet. What would that wretched cat do without you?"

The cat rolled on its back in front of the fire and watched with a curious green gaze as he drew her into his arms again.

Monsieur Duclos wished Yvette would be still for just a moment. The work-room was empty, she had sent all the girls away, but as he followed her about, begging and pleading, she picked up pins and put them away, examined materials, and shook out dresses and looked carefully at the seams.

"Oh, why will you not believe me," he cried at last. "I thought of nothing but you."

"I do not believe you," said Yvette flatly.

"I scrimped and saved so that we might marry."

"I have no proof of that." Yvette held a swath of silk up to the light and looked at it critically.

He pulled a notebook from his pocket. "See," he said. "See my accounts."

Yvette slowly put down the silk and took the book and carried it over to a lamp to read it. In the front of the book was written in French, "For my marriage to Yvette." Then there were the entries: the francs saved when he had walked instead of taking a carriage, the commission he had extracted from the wine merchant and the tailor in order to ensure that his master used their services, and a hundred other items.

"But," said Yvette, looking at him for the first time, "why did you not write to me? Why did you leave me that letter which only said goodbye?"

"In the first place, I did not know my own heart," he said humbly, "and in the second, I was afraid to write. I felt I had to see you in person. I told my master, and the comte said I must be patient and wait until he was ready to return to England on a visit. I wish us to be married, not only to right a great wrong, but because I love you."

"Could it be because you heard I was successful, I was rich?" demanded Yvette.

"I did not know it, I swear. My master says he will set us up in a little business in Paris. Think of it, Yvette. France. Home."

Yvette raised the lamp and studied his face, saw the anguish and pleading there. Then she carefully put down the lamp and said in a neutral voice, "Very well. Come, and I will introduce you to our son."

Tears of relief poured down Monsieur Duclos' face as he followed her from the work-room.

Effy Tribble was enduring a fit of silent rage. Harriet and Lord Charles had returned together to tell of their adventures and to break the news of their engagement. At first, Effy was as delighted as Amy, but then Harriet had said, "We will have a double wedding, Miss Amy, for I would be proud to share your great day," and Amy had cried and embraced Harriet.

Then there was worse to come. A radiant Yvette arrived on the arm of Monsieur Duclos to announce *their* forthcoming wedding, and what must that fool of an Amy do but suggest they, too, got married on the same day.

Mr. Randolph was dancing attendance on her, and Effy could have slapped him.

At last, she could not bear it any longer and said in a thin voice, "Mr. Randolph, will you follow me? I have something to say to you."

Mr. Randolph rushed to open the door as Effy tripped out. She led him to the morning-room, and then turned to face him.

"What do you wish to say to me, Miss Effy?" he asked.

"I think the question should be, Mr. Randolph, what have you to say to *me?*"

Mr. Randolph scratched his head. "I know!" he said after a moment's hard thought. "So many weddings! You wish me to help with the arrangements."

Effy sank down gracefully into a chair and closed her eyes. "Go away," she said faintly.

Mr. Randolph did not appear to have heard. He was pacing up and down the room. "Of course, it will be a crowded day," he said. "And so many guests! Thank goodness, I do not have many relatives. If you wish to be married on a different day to Miss Amy, you have only to say so."

Effy opened her eyes.

"Do you mean you wish to marry me?"

Mr. Randolph stopped his pacing.

"Yes, my love, heart of my heart."

Effy thought of all the long years, years full of dreams of a proposal of marriage. It must be done properly or not at all.

"If you wish to marry me," she said coldly, "you must propose properly."

"You mean . . . ?" Mr. Randolph looked down at her in dawning surprise.

"Yes," said Miss Effy Tribble sternly. "Down on your knees, Mr. Randolph!"

Chapter 8

*Marriage is popular because it provides the
maximum of temptation with the maximum of
opportunity.*

—*George Bernard Shaw*

OR A WHILE LONDON society
talked of nothing but the Tribbles.
Not only had they secured a matrimonial prize for their
provincial charge, but had gained rich husbands for themselves. And then the Duke and Duchess of Berham wrote
to say they were being married again, this time in church,
and would the Tribbles be guests of honour?

Dizzy with love and success, Amy grew noisy and out-
rageous. She was even beginning to strain the patience of
Mr. Haddon when, fortunately for him, disaster fell.

Amy needed to be brought down to earth and it was
one little bottle of hair dye that did it.

One evening, she locked herself in her room after an-

151

nouncing that she had a surprise for everyone. When she did not emerge the next day, Effy and Harriet grew anxious and became even more anxious when Amy did not respond to their calls and when they found the door of her bedchamber locked.

The gentlemen were sent for—Mr. Haddon, Mr. Randolph, and Lord Charles.

Harris produced a hammer from the kitchen and Lord Charles broke the lock and then the worried party crowded inside. The room was in darkness. The curtains were drawn and the shutters still closed. Amy could be dimly seen as a lump under the bedclothes, which were over her head.

Effy ran to the bed and tried to draw back the blankets, only to find her sister was holding them over her head in a ferocious grip.

Glad to find her alive, and becoming angry, Effy demanded, "What is this about, sister?"

A deep moan answered her.

Effy's voice softened. "Are you ill?"

"Go away," was the muffled reply.

Mr. Haddon eased Effy aside, seized the bedclothes and jerked them back.

The noise Amy made was rather like that of Lord Charles's cat when it had been stuffed in the leather bag. Mr. Randolph opened the curtains and pulled back the shutters and cruel sunlight flooded the room.

Amy looked a fright. Her face was blotched with tears and she had a hideous Kilmarnock nightcap pulled down over her ears.

She sat up and gave the assembled company a ghastly smile. "I had a bad dream," she said. "Please leave and allow me to dress."

Effy's eyes narrowed as she surveyed her sister. She felt

she could never forgive Amy for having become engaged first and crowing about it. When they went on calls, Amy never failed to point out that fact.

And then she saw a little tendril of hair escaping from under that nightcap, hair of a peculiar colour.

Bending over Amy as if to arrange the pillows, she seized the cap and pulled it off.

Mr. Randolph let out a squawk of laughter and Lord Charles turned away to hide a smile.

For Amy Tribble's hair was bright orange, like a fiery sunset, like a clown's wig.

"Oh, Amy," breathed Effy, trying to keep the satisfaction out of her voice. "You do look a fright."

Harriet's voice rang out. "Leave me with Miss Amy," she commanded. "Go away, all of you, and that includes you, Miss Effy. Harris, fetch Monsieur André, the hairdresser, and get him to come here immediately.

"Now there is nothing even you can do with that head of hair, my love," teased Lord Charles as Harriet shooed them all away.

"No, there's nothing," echoed Amy miserably when she was alone with Harriet. "What an old fool I am!"

"Why did you do it? You looked very well as you were," said Harriet.

"The ladies would say things, you know, when we were out on calls. Even the Marchioness of Raby kept going on about how lucky we were, and that cat, Mrs. Gilchrist, said loudly I must be a witch because most women of my age were dead and hinted I must be very rich, otherwise Mr. Haddon would have looked for someone younger and prettier. And of course, so he could! What does he want with me? So I thought if I could get rid of the grey streaks in my hair, then I would look younger. Then I thought if I had fair hair, I would look even better. I went over to the City and an apothecary sold me the mixture, and may he rot in hell, the Bartholomew freak of a whoreson, and may his balls fall off into the kennel and may—"

"Miss Amy!" screamed Harriet, putting her hands over her ears.

"Well," sniffed Amy. "I am ruined."

"Nonsense," said Harriet, lowering her hands in time to catch the last words. "We will both stay here until matters are rectified."

The house was hushed and quiet when the famous hairdresser arrived. He was ushered upstairs and treated by Effy more like a physician who has arrived too late to save a dying patient than a hairdresser.

There was no sign of Amy or Harriet for the rest of that day. Lord Charles, Mr. Haddon, Mr. Randolph, and Effy played cards in the drawing-room that evening. Effy felt that Mr. Haddon should be disgusted with Amy, but his lips kept curving in a smile, and little Mr. Randolph let out a snort of laughter every time Amy's name was mentioned. Lord Charles looked around the group and wondered why he should feel so much at home and so much at ease in such company. But his friend, Guy Sutherland, had started to make every excuse to call, and Lord Charles supposed, after some thought, that it was because, for all their nonsense, the Tribble sisters had managed to create a charming home.

The gentlemen left that evening without seeing Amy, but Harriet descended as they were putting on their coats in the hall and said Miss Amy would be happy to receive them the following afternoon.

Effy tried to see her sister before going to bed, but Amy's bedroom door was firmly locked, the lock having been repaired earlier that day.

On the following afternoon, all assembled in the draw-ing-room, and Harriet went to fetch Amy.

"A wig," said Effy. "That's the only answer."

And then Amy Tribble came in. She was not wearing a cap. Her long tresses had been cut, bleached, and then dyed a soft dark-brown. Soft waves and curls fell on either side of her face, softening its harsh lines, and her hair had been pomaded to a glossy sheen. She was wear-ing a morning gown of dull gold with a little Elizabethan ruff and long tight sleeves that ended in points at her wrists. She had never looked better. Effy could have slapped her.

Lord Charles drew Harriet aside. "You are beginning to frighten me, Capability Brown," he murmured. "Are you always going to solve every problem and leave nothing to me?"

But there was one problem facing Harriet and she could not tell him about it. She was frightened of the intimacies of the marriage bed and felt she had no one to turn to; the Tribbles, she assumed correctly, both being virgins.

It never crossed her mind that the Tribbles should be plagued by similar fears, and not one of the ladies dreamt that both Mr. Randolph and Mr. Haddon were becoming increasingly worried and for the same reason. For the two gentlemen were virgins as well.

Winter melted into spring and the day of the weddings approached, for all were to be married together, including Yvette and her Monsieur Duclos, but not the Berhams, who planned to be remarried at a later date. Lady Owen remained in Scarborough, writing to say she expected Harriet to bring her husband to see her, but she herself could not face the rigours of the journey south.

Mr. Haddon and Mr. Randolph were sharing a bottle of

wine in their favourite coffee-house when Mr. Randolph suddenly felt he could not bear his worries alone any longer.

"I have a confession to make," he said, blushing and looking down into his glass.

"That being?" asked Mr. Haddon.

"I am a virgin."

Mr. Randolph buried his nose in his glass.

"As a matter of fact," said Mr. Haddon slowly, "I, too, have no experience."

"We must remember our ladies have no experience either," said Mr. Randolph hopefully.

"But they will expect us to know what to do," pointed out Mr. Haddon dismally. "I declare I won't know which end is up."

Despite his distress, Mr. Randolph let out rather a coarse laugh.

"It's all very well to laugh," said Mr. Haddon, who was drinking steadily, "but is it fair to our ladies?"

"I don't really see how we can do anything about it." Mr. Randolph offered his snuff box but Mr. Haddon waved it impatiently away.

Mr. Haddon ordered another bottle of wine. Both men normally did not drink very much but that evening saw them becoming tipsy for almost the first time.

"Perhaps," said Mr. Haddon after the third bottle, "we should do something about it."

"Such as?" asked little Mr. Randolph owlishly.

"Lose it."

"Lose what?"

"Our virginity."

"With whores!" squeaked Mr. Randolph.

"There are whores and whores. I am not talking about the poor diseased creatures of the streets, forced by poverty into such circumstances. I mean the Royal Saloon in Piccadilly."

"Us go there! I should die of terror," said Mr. Randolph.

"Better to die of terror there than die of terror on our marriage beds."

They drank and argued and drank and argued until suddenly, feeling elated and courageous and not at all like himself, Mr. Randolph said, "I'll do it."

In a booth behind them, Mr. Lawrence slowly lowered his newspaper and smiled. A most fascinating conversation. He had never forgiven Mr. Haddon for challenging him to a duel. He summoned the waiter and asked for pen, paper, and ink and began to write.

Amy and Effy were preparing to leave the drawing-room and go to bed. Both of them wondered what had happened to their beaux that evening. Harriet was sitting by the fire, reading. Lord Charles had introduced her to the world of fiction and now she felt she could not read enough.

Amy cocked her head. "I wonder who that can be hammering at the street door. It is nearly midnight."

Harriet put down her book. "It might be the watch," she said. "Perhaps Harris left the basement door open."

"Harris would never do that," said Amy. "He is most careful. Oh, here he comes."

Harris handed a letter to Effy. It was addressed to both sisters.

"I wonder who it can be from," said Effy, turning the letter over in her hands.

"Well, open it and see," said Amy impatiently.

Effy broke the plain seal and began to read. Her eyes grew rounder and rounder with alarm. Amy could bear it no longer. She snatched the letter out of Effy's hands. Harriet watched her face turning grim and set.

"Who is it from?" cried Harriet.

Amy silently handed her the letter. "Dear ladies," she read. "If you wish to know how your fiancés pass their nights, go to the Royal Saloon."

"What is the Royal Saloon?" asked Harriet.

"A brothel in Piccadilly," snapped Amy.

Harriet laughed. "It is a malicious lie. How can you believe such spiteful nonsense?"

Amy looked at Effy and Effy looked at Amy. "I don't know about that," said Amy. "But I'm damned well going to find out."

Effy's pretty crumpled face had taken on a cold, hard look. "I shall go with you, sister."

"Then you will take me," Harriet closed her book with a snap. "You are not going to such a place alone."

"Yes, we are," said Amy sternly. "You will do as you are told, Harriet Brown, and stay here and wait for us."

Harriet pleaded and argued, but the sisters would not listen to her.

Lord Charles Marsham was enjoying a quiet glass of brandy when he was informed by his surprised butler that his fiancée had called.

"Show her in," he said, wondering anxiously what adventure had befallen Harriet now.

He listened in amazement as she told him of the Tribbles' visit to the Royal Saloon. "So we must go too," begged Harriet.

"I will go, my dear girl, but you must not."

"I am going. If it is true, my ladies will need comfort and help."

He hesitated a moment and then said quietly. "Very well. I must insist, however, that you wear a mask. In fact, I shall lend you a domino. But I must say I find it hard to believe that either Haddon or Randolph could be in such a place."

They arrived just after the Tribble sisters had made their entrance, their coachman having wasted a great deal of their time in trying to persuade them not to go in.

The Royal Saloon's busiest hours were between midnight and dawn. It was decorated in what the proprietors fondly believed was the eastern style. There was a main room and along either side of this were curtained recesses for private parties. The balcony, decorated with trellis-work and palms, also had a series of these semi-private boudoirs, and at the back were card-rooms and a billiard-room.

A large part of the peerage was present every night, and when the Tribbles strode in, earls, dukes, lords, and marquesses pushed aside their Cyprians and dived for cover under the tables. Most were married, and most of their wives were known to the Tribble sisters.

Amy's eyes raked the room. Then, followed by Effy, she went around the recesses, jerking back the curtains, deaf to the screams of the couples revealed.

"I've never seen so many bare arses in my life," grumbled Amy, making for the balcony. Effy was quite white and was beginning to feel she might faint. Along the balcony strode Amy, jerking aside the curtains, just as Lord Charles and Harriet entered downstairs.

Harriet knew the Tribbles had found their quarry. There was a piercing scream from the balcony from Effy, a cry of "Bastard!" from Amy, and then both Tribbles descended, their heads high.

"Come, Harriet," said Amy, recognizing her despite the

scarlet domino that shrouded her and covered her face, for she saw Lord Charles beside Harriet and, despite her own disillusionment, knew that Lord Charles was too much in love with Harriet to be unfaithful to her with any whore. "I told you not to come."

Harriet and Lord Charles followed them out.

"Please bring Miss Brown home," commanded Amy, her stare fixed, not looking at either Harriet or Lord Charles. The sisters entered their carriage and were driven off.

"We cannot go home," said Harriet. "We must go back in there and find out what happened. They must be doing it for some sort of wager."

"I do not have your faith in the good intentions of men," said Lord Charles, "and no, you are not going in there."

Harriet rounded on him. "Did you not see them? The Tribbles? Their lives are blighted. If there is some reasonable explanation, then we must discover it."

At that moment, Mr. Haddon and Mr. Randolph came out of the Royal Saloon, arm in arm.

Harriet flew at them before Lord Charles could stop her. "How could you?" she raged.

"We cannot explain such a delicate matter here, Miss Brown," said Mr. Haddon.

"Then where can you explain it?" demanded Harriet fiercely.

Lord Charles joined them. "We will take you home, Harriet, and then I shall find out what I can. No! You have been allowed too much license for one evening. Do you think these gentlemen will talk easily in front of you?"

Harriet reluctantly accepted the wisdom of what he said. She was returned to Holles Street and Lord Charles drove off with the nabobs.

Amy and Effy were in the drawing-room, drinking port. Their faces were flushed and their eyes hard. Tomorrow, tears would come, but that night they were in the middle of the battlefield of life and fighting their shattering disappointment with every bit of courage they had.

"Lord Charles has gone off with them to demand an explanation," said Harriet.

"More fool he," said Amy. "And more fools us. Men are not worth a whistle, Harriet. Help yourself to port and do not mourn for us. We had a lucky escape."

"But what were they *doing?*" wailed Harriet. "I mean were they . . . ?"

"They were the only ones who weren't, I'll grant you that," said Effy waspishly. "They were sitting with a couple of the lowest bawds and drinking champagne."

"With . . . with all their . . . em . . . clothes on?"

"Yes."

"Well . . ."

"Well, nothing," snapped Amy. "They just hadn't got around to removing their breeches."

"And to think," said Effy, "that I have been so frightened of the intimacies of marriage."

"You too?" said Harriet. "But it is not the same for you."

"Why not?" demanded Amy.

"You are older, and . . . and I saw you pulling back those curtains and heard the screams. After what you saw . . ."

"Seeing's one thing, doing's another," said Amy. "Take a wrong turning in a wrong part of London and you'll see the same thing. Maybe it's all the same when it comes to between the sheets, whores and ladies alike."

"But we have love and respect," protested Harriet.

"Had," said Amy gloomily. "Had."

"But I thought," ventured Harriet after a long silence,

"that many men behave thus after marriage and ladies turn a blind eye."

"I thought so too," said Amy, "and I always thought I could do the same thing, but I couldn't. Not me."

She crossed the room and sat on the sofa beside her sister and put an arm around her slim waist. Effy sighed and leaned her head against Amy's shoulder. "Perhaps this is God's way of punishing us," said Effy. "We were so very happy. So very triumphant. Too much pride and vanity."

"I do not believe God punishes anyone," said Harriet.

"Strange words coming from the daughter of a Methodist," said Amy.

"I cannot believe that a loving God punishes," said Harriet firmly. "I believe we punish ourselves."

"You stick to your beliefs and we'll stick to ours," snapped Amy. "It is not my fault that they prefer to lift the skirts of diseased mutton."

This last coarseness had the effect of silencing Harriet, but yet she felt she could not abandon them and go to bed. If the situation could be saved, then Lord Charles would save it. He was a good and competent man.

An hour later, there came a banging on the street door. Ignoring Amy's cry of "Don't answer it!" Harriet ran down the stairs, unlocked and unbolted the door and swung it open. Facing her were Mr. Haddon, Mr. Randolph, and Lord Charles.

"Put these gentlemen in the downstairs saloon, my sweet," said Lord Charles, "and then show me up. And leave me with the sisters, Harriet. What I have to say is private and not for your ears."

He expected protests from Harriet, but she merely nodded, ushered the gentlemen into the saloon, and then went downstairs to the kitchen to find them something to drink, the servants having all gone to bed.

Mr. Haddon and Mr. Randolph sat looking like guilty schoolboys. They waved away the wine, and Mr. Randolph asked feebly for a glass of seltzer instead.

Upstairs, Lord Charles, having finished his explanation with "So you see, ladies, they had already decided just to drink their champagne and leave without getting up to anything," discovered that doing good had ample reward, and the reward was the slowly dawning sunrise in the sisters' hitherto miserable and haunted eyes.

"Do you mean to tell me," asked Amy in an awed voice, "that they are *both* virgins?"

"Very much so. And so devoted to you both, they felt it not fair of them to take you to bed without experience, but that experience of the brothel so disgusted them that they decided to forgo it."

"It's very sweet," murmured Effy drunkenly, "to think of us all being virgins together."

"Exactly." Lord Charles rose to his feet. "So may I now tell your beaux, who are waiting downstairs, that you have forgiven them?"

"Course," said Effy, drunk with wine and relief.

And so the gentlemen were ushered up. Harriet reflected it was an odd sight to see four people in their fifties holding hands and blushing shyly. Then Amy called for champagne and Harriet played waltzes on the piano, so badly that Lord Charles took her place and entertained the company.

And so they were all married at last, and what a day it was for London society. The streets around St. George's,

Hanover Square, were packed with sightseers. Members of society who had not been invited stood on top of their carriages to get a better look. It was, vowed the world at large, better than a public hanging.

All the Tribbles' previous young ladies had turned out in force with their husbands—Felicity and Fiona, Delilah, Clarissa, and Maria.

The only sad member was a widow in black on the edge of the crowd—Bertha, Frank's wife and the Tribbles' ex-maid. Curiosity had drawn her to see what she could of the wedding. Frank had left their savings with her before he went to London and to his death, so she was comfortably provided for. But she felt a superstitious fear of the Tribbles and decided at last to move away from the vicinity of the church in case they saw her and put a curse on her.

Effy and Amy were the first to arrive, and then, in a carriage behind them, Harriet and Yvette. Effy had to be forcibly persuaded from turning out in an unsuitable white gown and veil and was dressed instead in floating blue chiffon. Amy was very grand in gold lace and with a cap of gold sequins and pearls on her head. Harriet was in white satin and Brussels lace and Yvette in a severe grey silk gown with a white ruff of stiffened gauze at her throat.

Several peers disgraced themselves by jumping to their feet and cheering as the sisters entered the church. Whether this was caused by admiration or by the sheer relief that the sisters had kept their mouths firmly shut over who had been at the brothel that night was not quite clear.

Effy paused nervously as she saw the aisle stretching out in front of her, all the long way to the altar.

"I cannot believe we are here at last," she whispered.

"Yes, here we go," said Amy and, grasping her sister's arm firmly, she began to move down the aisle.

It was a long ceremony. Outside, people played cards or bought gingerbread and oranges from the hawkers. And then the bells began to peal and the church doors were flung open and two radiant Tribble sisters stood on the steps with their husbands as the roar of the crowd engulfed them.

Their wedding had caught everyone's imagination. Love did not die and no one was ever too old to find it. Harriet, beautiful and blushing and the perfect bride, was ignored as the crowd surged cheering after the Tribbles' carriage.

Lord Charles's father, the Duke of Hambleshire, had opened up his town house to provide room for the great reception. There was an enormous banquet with lengthy speeches, and some elderly people fell asleep, and some overexcited, overstuffed children were sick under the table.

Harriet was conscious of an increasing feeling of nervousness. It was all very well for the Tribbles to contemplate their wedding night with equanimity. *They* were going off to bed with their virgin husbands while she would be alone in the company of a highly experienced man. Lord Charles had finally told her what Mr. Haddon and Mr. Randolph had been planning to do on their visit to the brothel.

Too soon for Harriet was it time for the couples to take their leave. She took a tearful farewell of the sisters, hugging them fiercely, and wishing all in that moment she could return to Holles Street and have a quiet evening alone with her books.

Lord Charles gave her a glinting, mocking look when they were alone in his carriage. "The sooner I get you to bed, the better."

Harriet blushed. "Why?"

"You are suffering from an acute case of bride nerves."

Harriet plucked nervously at the skirt of her gown. "I gather," she ventured, "it is quite common for some ladies and gentlemen to wait a few years after their marriage before . . ."

"Not in our case."

Harriet turned her face away and blinked back sudden tears. She felt very alone in the world.

They reached Lord Charles's town house all too soon. The staff were lined up in the hall to greet the new bride. Tom, the cat, had to be petted and fussed over. Then they walked up the stairs. "This is my bedroom here," said Lord Charles, "and this, across here, is yours."

Harriet smiled with relief. "In that case," she said timidly, "if you will excuse me, I will go to bed, for I am very tired."

"Go ahead," he said, kissing her lightly on the forehead.

Harriet smiled to herself as she undressed. It was all much simpler than she had imagined. They would get to know each other better, and then, perhaps in a year's time or something like that, they could . . . get down to business.

She climbed into bed and blew out the candle and settled herself for sleep.

The next thing she knew was that someone was climbing into bed with her.

"Charles!" she wailed, suddenly wide awake.

"Yes, Harriet," he said, pulling her into his arms. Oh, *yes,* Harriet."

And at his touch, all Harriet's passion took over from her fears, so that when he at last paused to remove her night-dress, she could hardly wait for all the love-making to recommence.

The members of the house in Holles Street, who had all successfully lost their virginity the night before, were tired but smug the next day, each one feeling proudly that a man or woman with twenty years' sexual experience could hardly have done better.

They all met for breakfast at noon, blushing shyly and giggling as if they were sixteen.

The gentlemen then went off to their club and the sisters surveyed each other with satisfaction.

"We've done it, Effy," said Amy. "We're married ladies, by George."

"Mr. Randolph is so devoted to me," sighed Effy. "I hope it does not disturb you, sis. Mr. Haddon always appears a leetle—shall I say?—cold."

Amy grinned. "He's as hot as a furnace, dear."

Effy blinked. "Sister, dear, I did not like to tell you yesterday, but your hair is showing grey at the roots."

"Slut on you!" roared Amy. "You whining, jealous, poisonous viper."

Effy began to cry, and Amy, immediately contrite, put an arm around her.

"There, I am a brute, Effy, and we should not quarrel now we have everything we want. And it's goodbye to the school for manners."

"Thank goodness for that," said Effy cheerfully, her tears, as usual, drying like magic.

OCT   1990